With Valentine's Day, February is always a romantic month. And we've got some great books in store for you....

The High-Society Wife by Helen Bianchin is the story of a marriage of convenience between two rich and powerful families.... But what this couple didn't expect is for their marriage to become real! It's also the first in our new miniseries RUTHLESS, where you'll find commanding men, who stop at nothing to get what they want. Look out for more books coming soon! And if you love Italian men, don't miss *The Marchese's Love-Child* by Sara Craven, where our heroine is swept off her feet by a passionate tycoon.

If you just want to get away from it all, let us whisk you off to the beautiful Greek Islands in Julia James's hard-hitting story *Baby of Shame*. What will happen when a businessman discovers that his night of passion with a young Englishwoman five years ago resulted in a son? The Caribbean is the destination for our couple in Anne Mather's intriguing tale *The Virgin's Seduction*.

Jane Porter has a dangerously sexy Sicilian for you in *The Sicilian's Defiant Mistress*. This explosive reunion story promises to be dark and passionate! In Trish Morey's *Stolen by the Sheikh,* the first in her new duet, THE ARRANGED BRIDES, a young woman is summoned to the palace of a demanding sheikh, who has plans for her future.... Don't miss part two, coming in March.

See the inside front cover for a list of titles and book numbers.

Harlequin Presents®

GREEK TYCOONS

They're the men who have everything— except brides...

Wealth, power, charm—
what else could a handsome tycoon need?
In THE GREEK TYCOONS miniseries you
have already met some gorgeous Greek
multimillionaires who are in need of wives.

Now it's the turn of popular Presents author
Julia James, with the attention-grabbing romance
Baby of Shame

This tycoon has met his match, and he's decided
he *has* to have her...*whatever* that takes!

Coming in May 2006
The Greek's Bridal Bargain
by Melanie Milburne
#2538

Julia James

BABY OF SHAME

GREEK
TYCOONS

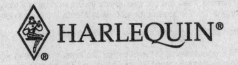

HARLEQUIN®

TORONTO • NEW YORK • LONDON
AMSTERDAM • PARIS • SYDNEY • HAMBURG
STOCKHOLM • ATHENS • TOKYO • MILAN • MADRID
PRAGUE • WARSAW • BUDAPEST • AUCKLAND

ISBN 0-373-12518-6

BABY OF SHAME

First North American Publication 2006.

Copyright © 2005 by Julia James.

This edition published by arrangement with Harlequin Books S.A.

® and TM are trademarks of the publisher. Trademarks indicated with ® are registered in the United States Patent and Trademark Office, the Canadian Trade Marks Office and in other countries.

www.eHarlequin.com

Printed in U.S.A.

All about the author...
Julia James

JULIA JAMES lives in England with her family. Harlequin® novels were the first "grown-up" books Julia read as a teenager, and she's been reading them ever since.

Julia adores the English countryside (and the Celtic countryside!), in all its seasons, and is fascinated by all things historical, from castles to cottages. She also has a special love for the Mediterranean. She considers both ideal settings for romance stories! Since becoming a romance writer, she has, she says, had the great good fortune to start discovering the Caribbean as well, and is happy to report that those magical, beautiful islands are also ideal settings for romance stories! "One of the best things about writing romance is that it gives you a great excuse to take vacations in fabulous places!" says Julia. "And all in the name of research, of course!"

Her first stab at novel writing was Regency romances. "But alas, no one wanted to publish them!" she says. She put her writing aside until her family commitments were clear, and then renewed her love affair with contemporary romances to great success.

In between writing, Julia enjoys walking, gardening, needlework and baking "extremely gooey chocolate cakes"—and trying to stay fit!

PROLOGUE

'MR PETRAKIS.' His UK PA's voice was hesitant. 'Please excuse me for interrupting you, but—'

Dark, displeased eyes flashed up at her from the man seated behind the imposing mahogany desk. Maureen Carter quailed.

'I said *no* interruptions, Mrs Carter—for any reason whatsoever.' The deep, accented voice was brusque. For a fraction of a section the forbidding gaze admonished her, then simply cut her out of existence, returning to the papers spread out on the leather-topped surface of the desk.

In the doorway, Maureen Carter hesitated, then, visibly steeling herself, spoke again.

'I understand, sir. But...but she said the call was urgent—'

Alexis Petrakis sat slowly back in his large chair and lifted his eyes to her.

'Mrs Carter,' he said, and his voice, with its slight Greek accent, was soft—so soft it raised the hairs on his PA's neck. 'You may inform Natalia Ferucia I have no interest in her affairs. With me or with anyone else.'

He rested his killing gaze on her, his mouth whipped to a tight, hard line, and then once again he returned to the papers on his desk.

His PA swallowed and cleared her throat. 'Mr Petrakis—' she attempted a third time '—it isn't Ms Ferucia on the line. It's a Mrs Walters, from Sarmouth Social Services Department. She says it's very important to speak to you,' she added quickly, as Alexis Petrakis stilled and lifted his head again. His dark eyes levelled on her.

'It's in connection, she says, with Rhianna Davies.'

For one long second the gaze levelled on her went completely blank, as though the name she had just given him was as unknown to him as it was to her. And then a mask closed over his powerful, planed face.

'Tell this Mrs Walters, whoever she is,' he enunciated, cutting each word out of the air as if he were vivisecting it with a scalpel, 'that I have no interest whatsoever in Rhianna Davies.'

He picked up his gold pen and returned to his papers.

'But, Mr Petrakis,' Maureen Carter said, with a final desperate urgency, 'Mrs Walters says it's about your son!'

And this time, finally, she got a reaction.

Alexis Petrakis froze.

CHAPTER ONE

RHIANNA was stepping out on to the zebra crossing. It was pouring with rain, the wind battering the rain hood on Nicky's buggy. She'd checked both ways before starting to cross, but as she pushed forward, eyes stinging with rain, her head bowed into the wind, weak and exhausted but with desperate urgency, it came again, the way it always did.

A screech of tyres, an engine roaring, and then a blow so violent it lifted her up and threw her sideways as the black and white painted tarmac slammed up to meet her. And then the sickening thud of her body impacting—and then the darkness. Total darkness.

She jerked as her brain relived, yet again, the moment when the speeding car had run her down on a pedestrian crossing. The jerking caused pain, shooting through her, but following the pain came worse—much worse.

A voice screaming—screaming inside her head. Distraught. Demented.

Nicky! Nicky! Nicky!

Over and over again. Drowning her with terror and fear and horror. Over and over again—

A hand was on her shoulder. Her eyes flew open. One of the nurses was speaking.

'Your little boy is safe—I've told you that. He's safe. He wasn't injured.'

Rhianna stared up into the face looking down at her, her eyes pools of anguish. 'Nicky,' she whispered again, her voice husky, fearful. 'Nicky—where are you? Where are you?'

The nurse spoke again, her voice calm and reassuring. 'He's being looked after until you get better. Now, you just relax and get some sleep. That's what you need now. Would you like something to help you sleep?'

Rhianna pressed her lips together and tried to shake her head. But any movement when she was awake was agony. Even breathing was an agony, her infected lungs raw and painful.

'I can't sleep—I mustn't! I've got to find Nicky…they've got him. They won't give him back. I know they won't—I know it, I know it!'

Her voice was rising again, fear gulping in her throat, and she could hardly get the air out of her.

'Of course you'll get him back,' the nurse said bracingly. 'He's only been taken into care while you're here. As soon as you come out they'll hand him over—'

But terror flared in Rhianna's eyes.

'No—she's taken him. That social worker. She said I couldn't look after him, that he'd be better off in care.' Her hand clawed at the nurse's fingers, eyes distending. 'I've got to get him back. He's my son!'

'I'll get you a sedative,' the nurse said, and went off. Dread and anguish filled Rhianna. Nicky was gone. Taken into care. Just like the social worker had said he would be.

'You clearly can't cope with looking after a child.' Rhianna heard the condemning tone ringing in her memory. 'Your son is *at risk.*'

Oh, God—why? Why? thought Rhianna. Why had the woman had to turn up just then? She'd felt so *ill,* and it had only been a few days after her father's funeral. She'd taken a double dose of flu powder and it had knocked her out, so that when the social worker had arrived it had been Nicky— still in his pyjamas, patiently watching toddler TV in the living room, with a bowl of spilt cereal on the floor—who'd opened the door to the woman while his mother lay collapsed in bed, breathing sterterously and all but unconscious…

The woman had taken against her, Rhianna knew, the first time she'd ever come to the rundown council flat to assess whether Rhianna's plea for home help for her father was valid or not. The woman had told Rhianna bluntly that her father needed hospitalisation until the end came, that a dying man should not be anywhere near a small child, and that if Rhianna insisted on refusing to name her child's father she had no business expecting the state to pay for his upbringing instead of his father. Nicky should be in nursery and she should go back to work, because that was government policy.

At the end of her tether, Rhianna had lost her temper and yelled at the woman, not registering that she was still holding the vegetable knife she'd been chopping carrots with in the kitchen before the social worker had come in to harangue her. Seeing the knife blade, the woman's eyes had flared, and she told told Rhianna she was dangerously violent and brandishing a weapon threateningly.

After that everything had gone increasingly downhill. Her father's life had drawn to its tormented close, and she'd eventually had to call an ambulance to take him to hospital, where a final stroke had brought the end at last. Her exhaustion, her illness, her desperate need to shelter Nicky from what was happening all around him, had laid her lower than she had ever been in the five bleak years since her world had collapsed around her.

And when the social worker had arrived that fateful morning, to find Nicky unsupervised and Rhianna passed out, it had been the final straw.

'I'm having a Care Order issued,' the woman had told her grimly. 'Before any harm comes to him either from your violent tendencies or your complete lack of responsibility.' She'd dipped her finger in the trace of flu powder on the bedside table and sniffed it suspiciously, glaring down at the barely conscious Rhianna. 'I'll take this for analysis, so don't even bother to try and hide whatever other drugs you've been using.'

She'd left the room, and Rhianna had somehow found the strength to get out of bed and stagger after her—only to crash into the doorframe as if she were, indeed, under the influence of drugs instead of being so ill with a chest infection she could hardly breathe.

When the woman had gone, informing her she would be returning shortly with the necessary documentation to remove Nicky, Rhianna, out of her mind with terror, had dragged clothes on and set off for the doctor's surgery, desperate to get some antibiotics as well as her doctor's avowal that she was not a drug user and was not violent—anything she could use to fight off the Care Order. But before she'd been able to get to the surgery she'd been knocked down by a speeding car on a pedestrian crossing.

When she'd surfaced back to consciousness it had been to find herself in a hospital ward, her body in agony, her limbs and torso strapped up, a drip in her arm and her lungs on fire.

And Nicky gone.

Nicky—her only reason for living, the only light in the black pall that crushed her, the only joy in her life.

Nicky—she had to get him back! She would die without him. And he—oh, God—she could not bear to think of his distress, his confusion. Taken into care with no familiar face around him, no mother to keep him safe the way she had kept him safe all his little life. Despite all the strain and pressure, the hardship and the relentless, punishing difficulties of nursing her difficult, cantankerous father, despite coping with no money, coping with her father's depression and his slow decline into both physical and mental incapacity, with no one to help, no one to turn to, and only the bare subsistence of the state to keep them going.

Nicky! The silent, anguished cry came again and again as she drifted in an out of consciousness, reliving over and over the moment when the car had crashed into her and she'd thought it was Nicky who'd been killed...

But he wasn't dead! Dear God she'd been spared that. He was alive, but gone, and she was terrified that she would never get him back. Never. He'd be put up for adoption, spirited away, locked away…taken from her…

The nurses had tried to help.

'Is there no one who could look after him for you? Friends, neighbours, relatives?'

Rhianna's hands had clawed on the bedclothes. 'No one.'

She had no relatives—not since burying her father. No friends left. All gone. And neighbours—she'd never befriended anyone in the council flats, too caught up in her own overwhelming problems to have time, or any spare energy, to notice anyone else—too horrified, if she faced up to it, that her life had sunk to these sorry straits.

One of the nurses had spoken again. Very carefully.

'What about your little boy's father?'

Rhianna's eyes had hardened automatically, irrevocably.

'He has no father.'

Tactfully, the nurse had said nothing more, but as she'd bustled off Rhianna's own words seared in her mind.

He has no father….

An image leapt in her mind like a burning brand.

Burning through her skin, her flesh.

Her memory…

CHAPTER TWO

RHIANNA had been desperate. Filled with a sick, agitated desperation that had made her do what she had done.

But she had had no choice.

Now, somewhere close to the hospital, she could hear the chilling wail of an ambulance siren. It echoed in her memory—the wailing siren of the ambulance, five long years ago, carrying her stricken father to hospital. A heart attack, and it had been her fault—her fault for telling him what she had just heard from Maunder Marine Limited. That they had themselves been acquired, and so their own corporate investment programme would have to go on hold until their new owners, Petrakis International, had given it their approval. That could take months, she'd been warned.

Months during which Davies Yacht Design would have no idea whether or not the life-saving takeover by MML would ever go ahead.

And without that assurance her father's company would go under—succumb to its debts as its creditors foreclosed. It would be the end of the company—and the end for her father. He lived for his company—lived for designing yachts. A vocation. An obsession. Taking over his whole life, giving it the only meaning it had.

And she, his daughter, would be no comfort to him.

Unless she could save his company.

She had left the intensive care ward, left her father wired up to monitors, the nursing staff looking grave, and gone back to her father's office.

And picked up the phone.

There *had* to be a way to get the go-ahead for the takeover by MML. She had been the one to approach them in the first

14

place, convincing the larger company that Davies Yacht Design was a profitable acquisition prospect. Forward order books were full, and the company's technical reputation was outstanding, but the chronic under-capitalisation and growing debt-interest burden, combined with a major client cancelling his already completed order and another one changing his mind halfway through, had pushed Davies Yacht Design to the brink. Her father's complete lack of interest in the mundane details of keeping a company financially healthy had meant the banks had lost confidence in him and they wanted an exit. If it wasn't going to come from a white knight like MML, then they would foreclose.

She *had* to get MML to go through with the acquisition!

But it had looked as if it was not on their say-so any more. It was Petrakis International who would have to agree to it.

And there was no reason why they should not, Rhianna had thought desperately. Investing in Davies Yacht Design would pay off handsomely—if she could just convince them as she had convinced MML.

But she'd hit a stone wall. It was standard corporate policy, Petrakis International had informed her, to stall all its acquired companies' major investments until they'd been checked out. She'd gone as high up the company as she could reach, and the answer had always been the same.

So she'd aimed for the top, as a last desperate throw.

Alexis Petrakis—head of Petrakis International.

Fifteen minutes. That would be all she'd need. Fifteen minutes to run through the figures, to show what a shrewd investment it would be for MML to buy Davies Yacht Design.

But his PA had shot down her hopes. Yes, Mr Petrakis was currently in London, but his diary was full, including the evenings, and he was flying back to Greece in three days' time. Perhaps next month…

But next month would be too late.

There had been only one thin sliver of hope left to Rhianna. The PA had mentioned that on his last evening in the UK Alexis Petrakis would be attending a business dinner at one of the top West End hotels.

It had been her last, last chance…

She closed her eyes, lying in her hospital bed, feeling memory pour over her like a sheet of acid, burning into her skin. Feeling again the claws, like pincers in her stomach, as they had that fateful evening as she'd sat worried sick, at the table in the thronged banqueting hall.

Because it had seemed Alexis Petrakis wasn't going to show! It had all been in vain. She'd come up to London, forked out a fortune for a ticket to the dinner, splashed out on a new dress and a session at the hairdresser and beauty parlour—all money she could ill afford, given the parlous state of the finances at Davies Yacht Design—all for nothing. She'd even altered the seating plan posted in the cocktail reception area for the dinner, so that she would be sitting next to Alexis Petrakis. But though she'd managed to take her seat without anyone else challenging her—the seat next to her, with Alexis Petrakis's nameplate—remained empty.

Her heart had sunk, heavy as lead.

If Alexis Petrakis were not there she might as well give up and take the next train home, to return to the hospital waiting room and wait for any sign that they would move her father out of intensive care.

Worry had closed over her.

A waiter had approached their table, deftly placing a starter course in front of each guest. As she'd murmured her desultory thanks another, taller figure, in a black jacket, not white, had suddenly also been standing there momentarily. Then he'd been taking his seat—right beside her.

'Do please excuse me—I've been delayed,' he apologised briefly to the table, his English fluent but accented. He nodded at several of the guests, acknowledging them by name, and then turned to his right.

'Alexis Petrakis,' he said, holding out his hand.

But Rhianna wasn't capable of responding. She was simply staring.

This *couldn't* be Alexis Petrakis. Alexis Petrakis—chairman of an international company—should be middle-aged and corpulent, like three-quarters of the male guests here tonight.

But the man who'd just joined the table was…*devastating*.

The word thudded in her brain.

He couldn't be much more than thirty, surely, with a whipcord leanness to him that was accentuated by the superb cut of his tuxedo—just as the dark tan of his face, his sable hair, were accentuated by the brilliant white of his dress shirt.

She gazed helplessly.

The planed contours of his face, the high, strong cheekbones, the straight nose, sharply defined jawline… And his mouth…

Sculpted, mobile, sensual.

She dragged her eyes upwards.

Straight into his.

Dark—obsidian-dark—but flecked very deep within with gold.

And looking at her—looking at her with total, absolute focus.

She felt weak, breathless.

Something flickered in those gold-flecked eyes.

'And you are…?'

The questioning voice was deep, with an accent that was making her toes curl in their narrow high-heeled shoes. There was faint speculation in the voice. She could hear it, and it quivered through her.

'Rhianna Davies,' she breathed helplessly, her eyes still speared by his.

She couldn't drag them away, just couldn't.

Numbly she placed her hand into his waiting one.

It was warm, with slight calluses on the pads below the finger joints.

He must work out, she thought, the words floating, dissociated through her.

The pressure of his grip was firm, but as he slid his hand

away there seemed to her to be the slightest, the very slightest, reluctance to do so.

Her insides were simply churning like a concrete mixer.

Then one of the other guests at the table addressed a remark to him.

For one last, brief moment his eyes held hers, and then they moved.

Rhianna's heart seemed to be pounding in her chest, thumping against her ribcage. Her blood seemed to be pulsing more strongly—which was weird, because she felt as weak as a kitten.

Alexis Petrakis. *That's* Alexis Petrakis....

She wanted to stare and stare...

Jerkily she forced herself to start eating. Fortunately the conversation at the table was between the other guests, and Alexis Petrakis was still addressing himself to the man who had spoken to him. Rhianna hadn't the faintest idea what they were talking about. The results of some company she'd never heard of—she caught snatches of words like 'interims' and 'EBITDA'. She ignored them. All she wanted to do—all she was capable of doing—was to go on gazing at Alexis Petrakis.

She had never, *never* set eyes on anyone so breathtakingly gorgeous.

She had seen her share of handsome men. Gone out with quite a few of them. She was lucky, she knew—very, very lucky—to have been blessed with a blonde beauty that had always drawn male eyes ever since she was an adolescent.

But her mother had kept her close, frightened she might, as she herself had done, fall disastrously for the first wrong man that came by. So for the most part Rhianna had contented herself with casual dating, keeping her admirers at bay. And since her mother's death in a car crash eighteen months ago she'd been in no frame of mind to look for romance.

Then there had been all the trauma of seeking out her estranged father and discovering the disastrous situation at his company to keep her from thinking about men.

So it was totally immaterial that Alexis Petrakis was the most stunning-looking male she'd ever set eyes on. Her only task was to persuade him to give the green light to MML's takeover. But that wasn't a subject she could broach in the middle of a formal business dinner. She'd always anticipated that she would have to use the dinner to give her an opportunity to request a private word with him after it was all over, and then go into her pitch.

In which case—she reached for her champagne flute—there couldn't be any harm in going on gazing at him, could there? While he talked to his business acquaintances...

She took a mouthful of champagne. It tasted warm. It had been poured out too long ago.

'Allow me—'

Alexis Petrakis had stopped his conversation. He was helping himself to the bottle of white wine left in its chiller by the wine waiter. As he took it out he glanced assessingly at the label, as if to check it was up to standard, and then filled Rhianna's white wine glass.

'Th-thank you,' she managed.

'My pleasure,' said Alexis Petrakis.

His long-lashed, gold-flecked eyes swept over her.

And Rhianna felt her stomach plummet all over again.

'Rhianna Davies,' the deep, accented voice murmured, as if searching private files inside his head. His eyes were still on her, and suddenly she felt a wash of liquid warmth go through her. With every inch of her consciousness she became aware of herself. Her silver gown, with the softly draped bodice and shoestring straps, her long pale hair flowing down her bare back, the wings of her hair caught with a silver clip at her nape, the silver necklace around her throat and the matching earrings she was wearing.

'You don't know me,' she got out,

'Not yet,' he murmured in reply, his eyes doing that weak-making wash over her again.

For a moment time seemed to stop. She just sat there, with

this extraordinarily magnetic man looking at her, and let herself be looked over.

While she looked back.

Deep, deep into his eyes.

Something flowed inside her. Something so powerful and overwhelming that her breath was ripped from her.

The rest of the meal was a blur. She must have made polite, general conversation, picked at her food, drunk her wine, but she couldn't remember a thing. The only thing she was aware of was the man sitting next to her. He talked to her sometimes, as the conversation meandered, but whenever he did she found herself almost completely tongue-tied.

The meal seemed to take for ever—and yet no time at all.

But as the after-dinner speaker finally stepped down, signalling the end of the formal proceedings, and conversation struck up again across the banqueting hall, Rhianna felt the pincers go to work in her stomach again. And this time it was because she knew that Alexis was the man—the only man—who could save her father's company.

And it was up to her to get him to do it.

Tonight.

Their table was breaking up. People were getting to their feet, taking their leave, either to leave the dinner completely or to mingle with guests at other tables. She mustn't let Alexis Petrakis leave! She had to keep him there. She had to do something. But how? She couldn't just blurt out *Please let MML buy my father's company!*

Then, just as she felt sick apprehension pool in her stomach, he spoke.

'May I offer you some port?'

Her head turned. Alexis Petrakis was reaching out to the port decanter. She watched him fill both their glasses.

She picked up her glass and sipped. The warm, rich liquid was like velvet in her throat.

Alexis Petrakis leant back in his chair. The gesture made the fine material of his dress shirt tauten across his chest, broadening his shoulders.

He had beautiful hands, she found herself thinking. Nails white against the olive tan of his skin. Long fingers.

She gave a hesitant smile. Her nerves were jittering. Any minute now he might glance at his watch, and murmur politely that he must go, or someone from another table might come up and start talking to him, cutting her out… She had to ask him now. And for her father's sake she had to get this right.

'Mr Petrakis—'

Her voice sounded high pitched. Where it had come from, she did not know.

She forced herself to go on. She had to.

'Mr Petrakis, I wonder—I wonder if I might have a word with you?'

Her eyes were wide—very wide.

Something changed about him. She didn't know what. But there was a sudden, instant edge of tension.

'In—in private,' she added.

Her voice was breathy.

For a moment his eyes were veiled, unreadable.

Oh, God, she thought. He's going to say no…

Then, slowly, he set down his port glass.

'Of course,' he replied. His eyes seemed to flicker over her, brushing like a very fine breath. He got to his feet. 'I'm sure,' he said, looking down at her, 'we can find somewhere sufficiently private.'

His voice was smooth, but it was like the smoothness of a sea where deep currents lurked beneath.

Her breath tight in her throat, Rhianna stood up.

He was tall, she realised. Towering over her five foot six. She paused to stoop and pick up her evening bag. Then, with her heart beating like a drum, she let him usher her from the banqueting hall.

As he steered her towards the bank of lifts in the lobby outside Rhianna paused and turned, looking up at the tall, overpowering man behind her. Her stomach was churning again, and she fought to subdue her nerves. Yet at the same time relief was surging through her. She'd done it—she'd got him to agree to listen to her. She had a chance—a last, last chance—to save her father's company.

Her father—lying in hospital, wires all over him, fighting for life…

'Mr Petrakis, thank you so much for agreeing to—'

'This way.' He cut across her careful speech with a murmur and ushered her inside a lift. Presumably they were going to the foyer, or one of the hotel's quieter bars.

But when the lift doors opened again they were on the penthouse floor. And the room whose door he opened with a single swipe of his electronic key was a suite.

For a second she hesitated. Then she crushed the feeling down. She needed to speak to Alexis Petrakis, and if he wanted to let her do so in his hotel suite then she was not about to object.

As she stepped inside and gazed around the suite's opulent reception room her eyes widened. What on earth must a suite like this cost for a night? Thousands of pounds? It must! The thought gave her courage—surely to a man worth as much as Alexis Petrakis buying up a small yacht design business would be peanuts.

She opened her mouth to speak, fumbling with the clasp on her evening bag so she could take out the sheet of paper that gave an at-a-glance summary of the business case she was going to put forward to justify the takeover.

But before she could open her bag she heard a soft 'pop' behind her.

She turned.

Alexis Petrakis was pouring champagne, filling up two flutes from the sideboard.

He strolled towards her.

There was something very controlled about the way he was walking towards her. It made her think, just for a second, of a wildlife film, with a leopard approaching the camera. It got closer, and closer—and then the shot cut out, as the cameraman retreated.

But she had no line of retreat.

She shook her head minutely. What was she thinking of? She didn't need a line of retreat. She just needed fifteen minutes of Alexis Petrakis's time.

She certainly didn't want champagne. But it seemed rude to reject it now that he'd opened a bottle specially—she tried not to think how much the hotel charged for champagne in the penthouse suite—so she took the proffered glass.

'Please—you shouldn't have—'

She sounded silly and immature. It was going to feel odd, she knew, putting forward a business case with a glass of champagne in her hand and wearing an evening dress, but she hadn't any choice. Besides, either the figures would convince Alexis Petrakis or they wouldn't. What she was wearing or drinking was irrelevant.

He was lifting his own glass.

'*Stin iya sas!*'

She looked blank.

'It is the equivalent of your "Cheers",' he said.

She gave a hesitant smile.

'I—I don't speak any Greek. I've never been to Greece.'

He raised his eyebrows. 'You have never been to Greece?'

'No.'

Her mother had not liked foreign travel. She'd liked to live in her little house in a small town in Oxfordshire, not going far. Nor had she liked the sea. She should never, Rhianna knew, have married a man whose obsession was designing ocean-going yachts. No wonder their marriage had broken up soon after she was born—even though her mother had always blamed her father for walking out on them.

'You should. It is one of the most beautiful countries on earth.' He strolled towards the sofa. 'Won't you sit down?'

Hesitantly she took a seat at one end, her narrow dress susurrating as she did so, depositing her handbag with its precious financial summary in it on the coffee table in front of the sofa. Alexis Petrakis set the champagne bottle on the coffee table and lowered his tall frame down on to the far end of the sofa. He rested the hand holding his champagne glass on the arm of the sofa; his other arm stretched out along the back of the cushions.

Disconcertingly close to Rhianna.

But then everything about Alexis Petrakis was disconcerting.

Disturbing to her peace of mind, making strange sensations ripple through her, making her body hyperaware of itself—of him.

Distracting to her concentration—which she needed to focus on how to put the business case for MML's takeover as persuasively as possible.

She didn't need to continually be stopping herself from just wanting to gaze and gaze at him...

Why couldn't he be fat and fifty?

She let her eyes flicker to him and promptly she wished she hadn't. Oh, God, he was just so fantastic-looking—she felt her heart begin to thump in her chest again. She took a draught from her champagne glass, trying to steady herself.

She took a deep breath.

'Mr Petrakis—' she began.

Again, her voice had come out breathy. She hated it. She needed to sound cool and composed and businesslike.

'Alexis...'

His voice was smooth. She didn't know what to answer. She didn't feel comfortable with addressing the head of a massive European business empire by his first name. And the low, accented pitch of his voice made a soft quiver go down her back...

Stop it! Just start telling him what you came here to tell him!

But he had started talking again.

'You really should go to Greece. There are many private places tourists hardly visit—if ever. This time of year, early spring, is especially lovely. The countryside is vivid with wildflowers before the heat of summer arrives. You would find it very beautiful.'

His voice was bland, but his eyes—Rhianna felt her throat tighten—were watching her with an expression that was anything but.

Nerves started to jitter inside her. She took another mouthful of champagne to steady them. The bubbles beaded in her mouth and she swallowed hastily. She could feel the alcohol giving her a jolt. Uneasily, she wondered how much she'd drunk that evening. She'd been careful, knowing how much was at stake, but even small amounts could add up.

And have an impact. Make her feel ultra-sensitive to things—ultra-aware. Make her misinterpret things.

Things like the way Alexis Petrakis was looking at her through dark, veiled eyes, relaxing back against the sofa cushions, casually lifting his champagne glass to his mouth…his mobile, sculpted mouth.

His sensual mouth…

For a moment she felt her gaze hang, unable to pull it away.

He did have the most incredible, sensual mouth…

With sheer effort of will she pulled her gaze away. Her mouth felt dry, despite the champagne she'd just drunk. She pressed her lips together, as if to moisten them.

His eyes narrowed. She saw it happen. Hardly at all, but discernible.

Hastily, she took yet another mouthful of champagne. It fizzed as she swallowed, and again she felt the alcohol kick through her. She took another breath, feeling her breasts lift as she did so.

'Mr Petrakis—'

Again that low-pitched, accented voice interrupted her.

'Alexis,' he corrected.

She pressed her lips again.

'Alexis.' She forced herself to say his name. It came out like a soft breath.

'Rhianna,' he replied.

The way he said her name was much more evocative than any way she'd ever heard it pronounced before. He took a mouthful of his own champagne. 'Rhianna,' he mused. 'It's not an English name I know.'

'It's—it's Welsh,' she said.

'How do you spell it?'

'R-h-i-a-n-n-a,' she spelt out.

He frowned. 'There seems to be a Greek ''rho'' in there.'

'I don't know,' said Rhianna, knowing she sounded stupid, but not knowing what else to say.

She didn't want to sit here discussing her name. Not when Alexis Petrakis was leaning back, champagne glass trailing from one hand, the other dangerously near her bare shoulder along the back of the sofa, one long leg crossed over his knee, looking supremely relaxed...

Or was he? She studied him covertly a moment.

He looked relaxed, but there was something about the way he was holding his body that made her think he was not. Not relaxed at all. As though a fine thread of tension were running through him.

Keeping him on a leash.

She felt her own body tense. Looking at him was a mistake. Every time she'd looked at him over dinner she'd felt that devastating weakness go through her, that tightness in her breath, that quickening of her heart-rate.

And she mustn't feel that. She just mustn't.

Suddenly she felt as if the walls of the room had moved in closer, crushing out some of the oxygen in the air. It was very quiet—the luxurious opulence had a deadening effect on sound, and the double-glazed windows let in no sound from the busy street far, far below.

With a tight intake of breath she made a third attempt to broach the subject she had to open.

'Mr—um—Alexis—' She stumbled over his name, still finding it hard to address him by his given name and not the more formal and honorific surname.

'Rhianna...' he echoed again. And again that was that slight quirk of his mouth, as though he found amusement in what she had just said.

He rested his eyes on her. Night dark, flecked with gold. If she looked long enough she could see the flecks quite clearly...

'Um—I just wanted to—to...'

Her voice was breathy again, and she hated it, but she couldn't make it sound crisp and businesslike. She was too wound up, too tense.

'Yes?' There was polite enquiry in his voice, and his expression was bland. But that thread of speculation was still there.

As if he's playing with me.

A prickle went down her spine.

She took another mouthful of champagne. It definitely helped, she thought.

'Tilt your glass.'

She blinked. He'd reached forward to pick up the champagne bottle on the table. Docilely, she found herself tilting her glass.

You don't need any more champagne!

Abruptly, she pulled her glass back. For the briefest second the golden effervescing liquid splashed on to her lap, before he straightened the bottle with a Greek expletive. The icy liquid soaked instantly through the fine material of her dress and made her cry out, and jolt, and then the frothing champagne was spilling out of her foaming glass, all down the bodice of her dress, just as icy.

She gave another cry.

'Oh, *no!*' she cried, appalled, jumping to her feet, gazing horrified at the soaked material. Champagne stained, she was sure of it—and, worse than that, the wet material was clinging tightly to her braless breasts, outlining them completely. Added to that, the cold of the liquid had had a predictable effect on her nipples, which were suddenly standing out like pebbles.

Mortified, she spread her free hand as concealingly as she could over her bodice, wanting the earth to swallow her. Abruptly, Alexis Petrakis—who was, she realised gratefully, taking the incident very calmly—removed the all-but-empty glass from her fingers.

'Perhaps you would like to go and change?' he suggested.

Rhianna's eyes flew to him. Was he being sarcastic or something? But she was in no position to care. And she realised he must just be trying to be as tactful as possible in a mortifyingly embarrassing situation.

He set down the champagne bottle and both flutes, and got to his feet.

'Let me show you where the bathroom is.'

'Thank you—I'm so—so sorry!' she gasped, her voice sounding breathy again, her eyes wide with embarrassment.

'Not at all,' was all he said, in a smooth, accented voice, as he tugged the light cord to illuminate the interior.

She dived inside and shut the door as quickly as she could. Her eyes flew to her reflection in the mirror over the huge basin, and she dropped her arms.

She had to get the champagne out fast, or it would stain. The dress had cost a fortune—she'd known she had to look as if she were an habitué of posh London business dinners—and she was loath to ruin it the first time she wore it.

Setting her teeth, she reached behind her and slid the zip hdown. It was soaked anyway—water wouldn't make it any wetter. She stepped out of the dress and caught her reflection in the mirror over the basin.

Her half-naked body looked…different.

Her breasts, still peaked by the effect of the cold champagne, were fuller, rounder. Her waist, accentuated by her suspender belt and skimpy briefs, seemed slimmer. Her legs, in their sheer stockings, more slender. Her hair, cascading down her completely naked back, much longer.

As for her face…

Smoky eyes looked back at her, deep set, with long dark lashes, her mouth, lipstick stained into her slightly parted lips, seemed lusher somehow.

She stared at herself

She looked…erotic.

The word stole into her mind, shocking her. She tried to push it away, but it was no use. She went on staring.

Everything, she realised slowly, was very slightly blurred, very slightly softened around the edges. She felt a creaming in her veins.

It made her feel…different.

And very, very aware of her body—her half-naked, erotic body—revealed in the mirror. And as she stared at herself she started to feel a tremor, deep inside her, as if something were stirring, had just awoken.

She pulled back. No, this was not on. Totally, totally not on.

Hastily she returned her attention to her wet dress. As she did so her eyes caught sight of the bathroom's courtesy hairdryer, tucked into its socket beside the basin. With relief, she seized it, spread out her dress over her free hand as much as possible, and turned the hairdryer on to it.

The thin material dried blessedly quickly, and without a stain. As she slipped the dress back on again it felt warm to her skin. She did up the zip, she checked her reflection again.

The heat from the hairdryer had brought a soft flush to her cheeks, a warmth to her exposed arms and shoulders. Her long hair had been lightly winnowed, lifted in silken strands. Again she felt that deep tremor stir within her, that creaming in her veins, that languor stealing through her.

What's happening to me?

She felt strange…dissociated. As if she were moving through a dream.

Slowly, she walked out of the bathroom.

And stopped dead.

Alexis Petrakis was in the bedroom.

He had discarded his tuxedo jacket, his dress tie was unfastened, as was the top button of his shirt, and he was slipping the gold links from his cuffs.

As she stepped out of the bathroom he looked up and across at her.

His eyes flicked over her gown. An expression of slight, mocking surprise lit in his eyes.

'Unnecessary. But...' he started to stroll towards her '...it has its compensations.'

It was the leopard again. Heading towards her.

But its leash had been slipped.

She couldn't move. Could only stand, totally frozen, her heart starting to hammer in great, pounding thuds that sent the blood rushing in her veins through all her body.

It was his eyes. She could see it in his eyes. See the gold flecks deep within. See the intent in them. The very, very clear intent.

Her lips parted, taking in breath. Instantly she could see his eyes narrow, that edge of tension tauten through him.

She had to move—but she was frozen. Completely frozen.

Waiting.

Helpless.

He stopped in front of her. She could feel his presence, invading hers. Catch the male musk coming from him, overlaid by the spiced notes of expensive aftershave.

He was looking down at her, out of those obsidian night-dark eyes, and she couldn't move—couldn't move. Could only gaze, helpless, up at him.

And drink him in. Drink in the sable hair, the lean planes of his face, the strong, straight cut of his nose, the faint masculine shadow along his jaw, roughening his smooth, tanned skin.

Oh, God, she thought. He is just so, so beautiful...

Her hand half lifted. She wanted to reach up, to cup her fingers along his jaw, feel the roughness of his skin, smooth her finger along the high arch of his cheekbones, reach with her mouth to his, feel the touch of it on hers. To slide her fingers into that silky sable hair and draw him to her, parting her lips...

She tried to stop herself.

But she couldn't. Had no power over herself any more.

She felt her body sway—sway towards him. She felt her hand lift, reach up…

He caught it. A swift, sudden movement that stilled her. His fingers closed around her wrist, pulling her towards him with slow, inexorable strength.

She gazed up at him, drowning.

His pupils were like pinpricks, flared with gold.

'Indulge me,' he said softly.

Her pupils dilated. She could not help it. Did not know it. Could only stand there, lips parted, wrist caught, her body swaying towards his.

'Indulge me,' he said again, more softly.

And then, with his other hand, he slowly, very slowly, slid one long finger underneath the thin strap over her shoulder and gradually, little by little, drew it down over her arm until he had peeled bare her breast.

'Ah, yes,' he said, his voice soft and low.

He let go her wrist and lifted his hand to the other strap. Drawing it down her shoulder, slowly peeling down the bodice of her dress.

She couldn't move. Not a muscle.

Could only stand while Alexis Petrakis bared her breasts.

For his delectation.

For one long, endless moment he just stood there, looking at her.

'You really are,' he said, in that same soft, low voice, 'exquisite.'

Beneath his gaze she felt her breasts prickle, felt them engorge, her nipples harden, tighten.

Felt the tremor deep within her quicken.

She felt her body sway again.

A small sound came from her throat. She did not know what it was. It was inchoate, unconscious.

But reality had stopped. Stopped the moment she had stepped out of the bathroom and set eyes on Alexis Petrakis, stood still while he advanced on her. With one purpose, one purpose only, in his tread.

He smiled now. His mouth curving.

'Yes,' he said, his lashes sweeping down over his dark, obsidian eyes. 'I know.'

He reached a hand to lightly, oh-so-lightly, stroke her hair. She felt a soft, trembling shiver go through her at his touch. The unformed sound came from her throat again.

Her breasts—swollen, taut—had begun to ache. A low, slow throbbing was resonating through her body. Her pupils distended, her body swaying forward yet again.

She wanted… She wanted…

His hand tightened in her hair, cupping her head.

She gazed at him, eyes huge, quite, quite helpless.

Something flared in his eyes—something that was instantly, ruthlessly leashed.

She went to his bed without a word, without a murmur. Only soft, aching moans that he could stop with his mouth. But when his mouth left hers to shape her breasts, to close over her straining, aching nipples, they came again. They came as he trailed his lips along the taut contours of her belly, as his palms smoothed her loosening thighs. And when his teeth grazed at the tender lobes of her ears, bit softly, so softly, at her swollen lip, the low, aching moans deep in her throat came again.

Reality fled. It was somewhere else. Another universe. A universe where pain and problems were, where worry and anxiety bit deep into the bones, where dread and fear pressed from all directions.

But here—here there was only bliss. Bliss such as she had never known, had never known existed.

How could the human body feel so much? How could the sense of touch be so exquisite? So all-consuming.

And how could she want more of it? And more, and more, and more?

Until her body was a single living flame, a flame that was burning, burning ever fiercer.

His body pressed her down. She felt its strength, its power.

Her hands revelled in the taut, sculpted muscles of his back, his shoulders. Her thighs strained against the sinewed cords of his. Against her belly she felt the long, hard shaft of his manhood.

A hunger started to grow in her. She writhed against him. His tongue was laving the swollen, aching peak of her nipple, sending flames shooting through her breast, making her fingers claw over his shoulders. From her throat tore the soft, aching moans she could not suppress.

She writhed against him again, the hunger mounting and mounting.

He smiled against her breast, lifted his head.

His dark eyes, flared with gold, looked down at her.

She felt the quickening pressure of his probing manhood.

Hunger bit through her again, fierce, unsated.

She twisted instinctively against him, feeling the pressure surge.

She wanted...

She gazed up at him, helpless, wanting.

'Yes,' he said softly. 'I know.'

The moan came from her throat again. Her eyes dilated, distended.

Pleading for what she wanted...

His features tensed, as if he were suddenly exerting a huge, overpowering control. Then, with slow, deliberate descent, he entered her.

Rhianna stirred. Her body felt heavy, languorous. She didn't want to wake. She wanted to stay within the dream she was having, enfolded within the circle of strong arms, clasped tight against the warm, hard body of the man cradling her in his sleeping embrace.

An embrace that had come only after an ecstasy so intense she had cried out, lips parting, throat arching, while her body writhed like a living, burning flame of bliss, on and on and on, until her whole being was one molten sheet of unbearable, exquisite sensation.

Only then, as the burning brand that was her body cooled to nothing more than a softly pulsing warmth, had he rolled back against the pillows in a fluid, exhausted movement, pulling her against him, folding her against his body. He had murmured something to her—she knew not what. Soft, sibilant words that were a breath in her ear. His hand had splayed possessively across her abdomen, his mouth warm against her shoulder.

She had felt weak with wonder, glowing with the last embers of the fire that had consumed her, warm and safe and sated.

She had slept a deep, deep sleep in the circle of his arms, her dreams capturing this moment of perfect happiness.

But now brightness was pressing on her lids, bringing her to reluctant wakefulness. She blinked open her eyes.

He was leaning over her. His eyes were heavy with desire. Deep within, they stirred her, warming the blood in her veins. Slowly he bent down to softly kiss her, his lips warm and tender.

'Good morning,' he said, his voice low, husky. 'I should ask you whether you slept well, but I happen to know...' long lashes swept over dark eyes '...that you slept very little last night.'

His gaze washed over her as she lay back against the pillows, her hair tumbled, her lips beestung from the night's long, long passion.

'You are even lovelier than you were last night.' The husk was thicker, and long lashes swept over his eyes again. 'I only wish...' His voice trailed off.

She gazed up at him, breathless, as he stood up.

He looked—breathtaking. He was freshly shaved, his hair very slightly damp from showering—and he was fully dressed in a business suit.

She felt a coldness start around her heart, a pooling of dismay nascent in her stomach.

He was looking at his watch, shooting back his cuff. He spoke again, but now his words were clipped, his voice terse.

'Unfortunately I have a business meeting this morning which I cannot avoid. So, much as I regret, I will have to leave you now.'

She heard the words, but for one dissociated moment she did not understand what they meant.

Then their meaning hit her with a sickening blow.

Oh, God, he was going—walking out.

She'd been taken for a one-night stand.

That was all it had been.

A convenient, handy, fast-food snack to stave off night starvation. He'd eyed her up, made his move on her, had sex with her, taken his fill, slept it off—and now he was going.

She felt sick. Reeling. And then, out of nowhere, another shockwave hit.

MML.

Horror galvanised her. Oh, *God*. This wasn't just *any* man she'd gone to bed with within hours of meeting him for the first time, who was now walking out on her in the customary brutal morning-after ritual. This was *Alexis Petrakis*—the one man in all the world who could stop her father's company going under...

And instead of getting him to approve the MML takeover, she'd fallen into bed with him—like a ripe, wanton peach.

Sickness drenched through her.

He was speaking again, drawing out a mobile phone from his inside jacket pocket.

'However, I will be—'

'No! Please—wait—don't go yet.'

He stopped speaking in mid-sentence.

'Rhianna, I—'

'No! Wait—please wait. There's something I must—something I wanted—'

She broke off. Oh, God—she had to do this. She would have given a million pounds not to, but she had to!

She pulled herself upright, clutching the sheet to her. Her heart was pounding. But she had to do this. However horrible it was to do it now...

'Before you go—there was—there was something I wanted to talk to you about!' She took a hectic breath. 'MML,' she said.

She stared at him wide-eyed, still clutching her sheet to her, her hair tumbled around her naked shoulders.

Alexis Petrakis had gone still.

'Go on.' His voice was controlled. Very controlled.

She swallowed. Forcing herself to speak. He'd told her to go on—she had to do so.

'You've frozen all its corporate investments. One of them is my father's company—Davies Yacht Design. I came to the dinner last night to meet you. To persuade you—'

'Yes?' The voice cut across her. 'To persuade me—?'

She stared at him. Something was happening to his face. The expression was draining out of it. Completely. Absolutely.

'Yes.' Her voice was breathy, her throat tight with nerves, her eyes distended. 'To persuade you to—'

Her voice broke off. A chill was starting through her. She could feel her skin contracting, tightening.

'To persuade you...' Her voice had husked to a low, breathy whisper. It was all she could manage. Her throat was stretched tight with nerves, with desperation, as she gazed up at him, her eyes wide with urgency. 'To go ahead with the takeover. It would be good for you—it really would. I promise. I can show you right now...'

Her voice trailed off, leaving unsaid the fact that she had a financial print-out in her handbag next door. There was something about his face that was frightening. Chilling her like ice.

Her heart started to thud as she stared up at Alexis Petrakis's expressionless face. Slowly he slid the mobile phone back inside his jacket.

'There is something you should know. You have made a mistake,' he said. And though his voice was soft, it was a softness that was deathly. 'A very bad mistake. You see...' He paused, and the eyes resting on her held, she realised, the same chill that was hollowing through her, were as expressionless as his face. 'I do not do business in bed. Ever. So, although you were very good—very good indeed—' his voice was a lacerating drawl, like a razor being drawn over her flesh '—you have used me for no purpose. Except, of course—' and now his eyes washed over her suddenly, and the expression in them made her gorge rise '—to demonstrate your...expertise. Exceptional expertise, in fact.' Long lashes swept down over his eyes, and when they swept back up again the obsidian gaze cut like a scalpel into her.

'You're very skilled, Rhianna, but you should have contented yourself with a cash payment. I'd have been happy to pay for you. In fact...' He reached inside his jacket again, but this time he took out a slim leather tooled wallet. He flicked it open. A cluster of fifty-pound notes fluttered on the bed. 'Keep the change,' he said softly.

Then he turned and walked to the door.

'You have ten minutes to vacate this suite. Hotel security will escort you out.'

At the entrance to the reception room he paused. He did not turn.

'As of now, MML no longer has any interest in Davies Yacht Design.'

His voice was hard. As hard as stone.

He walked out. He didn't look back.

In the bed, Rhianna started to shake.

CHAPTER THREE

'HE's in here.'

The woman opened a door off the narrow hallway. She had an infant balanced on her hip, tugging at her hair and whimpering, and an air of distraction about her that did not impress Alexis Petrakis.

Alexis controlled his emotions. He'd been doing that ever since he'd taken the call that his PA had patched through to him.

The call that threatened to change his life for ever.

It was only by the most stringent exercise of self-control that he had got to this point now. The moment of truth.

As he walked into the room, in front of the woman he felt his hands clench at his side.

Let this not be true! Thee mou, *let this not be true!*

Because it couldn't, *couldn't* be true. It couldn't be true what that social worker had told him over the phone That she had opened an envelope in Rhianna Davies's flat, as she was packing things for the child who had just been taken into emergency foster care, and read the handwritten note clipped to the boy's birth certificate—citing himself as father of her son.

Rhianna Davies was lying.

Christos, there could be no other explanation!

A woman like that—who had used him, had gone to bed with him to get his money—would not have hesitated a month, a week, to claim his paternity of a child she had conceived in that sordid encounter!

So she could only be lying. Lying to cause trouble...

Which meant that the child he was about to set eyes on could not *possibly* be his.

Dear God, please no—not his!

Alexis's eyes swept around the room. The carpet was strewn with children's toys. Two school-age children were sitting on a sofa, watching children's TV. Alexis felt his guts clench, and then release.

But even as he felt the cold start to drain out of his veins the woman began speaking in a deliberately low voice he could hardly hear above the blaring TV.

'He's not settled at all well. I've done my best, but he's just not responding. Poor little mite,' she finished, her distracted manner softening suddenly.

She walked in past Alexis and went up to a large armchair half hidden in this small room by the open door. Alexis felt his head turn to follow her as if it were filled with lead. Crouching down, rebalancing the infant on her hip slightly to do so, she said in a gentler voice, 'Hello, pet. How's tricks?' She ruffled the hair of the small child curled into the confines of the armchair, a battered teddy clutched tightly to him.

The child did not respond to the woman, either to her voice or her touch. He just went on sitting there, curled like a foetus, immobile, unresponsive. Tension in every line of his little body, his face averted so only his profile showed.

With a sigh she got to her feet. 'You see?' she said to Alexis.

He did not hear her. Did not see her. Saw nothing but the child curled into the chair.

His profile was familiar from a dozen family photo albums. Himself. Himself when young.

He could not move. His lungs were frozen, his body rigid. But emotion was knifing through him, blow after blow.

Killing him.

How long he stood there he did not know. Time had stopped.

Stopped five long years ago when his seed had melded with the woman who now, the social worker had told him, lay in a hospital bed. Just in time, she had told him, to make it so much easier to take the boy into care—away from such an irresponsible and unfit mother.

My son.

The words repeated inside his head over, and over again. *My son.*

Out of nowhere, overwhelming him, emotion poured through him. The fiercest, most overpowering urge to wrap that small, hunched body to him, to enfold him and protect him—*always.*

It shook through him, and he knew it for what it was. It was unasked for, but it had come all the same. And he would, he knew, be in its power all his days.

Slowly, very, very slowly, he started to walk forward, towards the little boy. At his approach the child tensed even more, his head turning fearfully. Dark, distended eyes stared up at him anxiously, his mouth trembling. Alexis felt his heart clench—with fury and with pain.

He forced a smile to his face. He must not, *must not* frighten the child.

'Hello, Nicky,' he said slowly, speaking to his son for the first time ever.

Rhianna stirred sluggishly, sleep draining from her. Her eyes opened heavily.

She stared, confused. She was no longer in a hospital ward. She was in a room on her own. The walls were a soft pink. A nurse was altering the slats of the Venetian blinds over the window.

'Hello,' she said brightly. 'How are you feeling?'

'Where am I?' Rhianna's voice sounded faint and dazed.

'You're in the Sellman Wing of the hospital. It's the private wing.'

'Private? But I can't afford—'

The nurse smiled reassuringly.

'Don't worry—everything has been taken care of. Now, tell me how you're feeling. You have a visitor, you know.'

Emotion leapt in Rhianna's eyes, completely obliterating the question of how she had come to be in a private ward.

'Nicky!' Her voice was a hoarse croak, and she started to try and sit up.

Immediately the nurse hurried forward to help prop her against the pillows, easing her skilfully back.

'Nicky?' she echoed.

Rhianna's eyes were strained and wide as she steadied her breathing after the effort of moving.

'My little boy,' she said, the pain in her voice audible.

The nurse stood back and shook her head regretfully.

'I'm afraid not. But if you're ready I'll send him in. He's been most impatient for you to wake.'

She bustled out.

Rhianna closed her eyes, desolation washing through her.

Nicky—he was her only thought. She had to get to him, find him, get him back. She didn't care if she could still hardly get out of bed, let alone walk, that her lungs still ached even through the painkillers, that her body still felt as if a steamroller had gone over it. She *had* to get home! Had to. Because how else could she get Nicky back?

Anxiety laced through her, fretting in every cell of her aching body.

The door started to open. Her eyes flew to it.

Who was it this time? Who could possibly be so impatient to see her?

The nurse had said 'him', so it couldn't be that awful social worker coming to triumph over her. So who, then?

As her eyes focussed on the man who walked in she felt for one sickening, hideous moment that she must still be asleep. Because she couldn't, *couldn't* be awake!

Shock buckled through her.

And horror. Deep, deep horror.

As if through a hole ripped out of time a man walked into

the room—from a past that came from her worst dreams, her sickest memories.

Alexis Petrakis had just walked in.

Alexis closed the door behind him and let his eyes rest on the woman lying in the bed.

What the hell—?

This wasn't Rhianna Davies. It was nothing like her!

Rhianna Davies had possessed a beauty so enticing that she had been able to make a fool of him as *no* other woman had ever done! Had made him feel— He couldn't now admit how she'd made him feel. She had been a woman who could have lured him to his doom if he hadn't found the strength of mind to throw her from him like a rotten fruit.

But her rottenness had been hidden beneath a surface so exquisite that he had been putty in her hands...

This woman looked like a death's head. Gaunt, her eyes sunken into their sockets, cheeks hollow, the bones sharp like a knife, and lines etched around her mouth. Her hair was lank, much shorter than it had been, straggling limply around her haggard face.

Involuntarily the image of the way he remembered her pushed into his mind—her body pulsing beneath him, her soft, lush curves, naked, wanton, sated.

And before that, in that silver evening dress, her hair like a silken fall, her eyes like smoke—promising everything, everything he wanted from her...

Something had punched through him the moment he set eyes on her at that dinner, five long years ago. Something he had never felt about a woman before. Never thought existed. He had wanted her instantly. Totally. More than any other woman he had ever wanted.

And for the chance to slake that overpowering, insistent wanting he had broken every rule in his book—just to possess her that very night as she'd offered herself to him on a plate.

And in the morning he'd discovered why she'd done so.

It had been another punch to his guts.

But quite, quite different.

He stared down at her now, hatred in his eyes.

This woman *couldn't* be the same one.

Thee mou, he'd known that she'd been taken into hospital after having been knocked down by a car, but that alone couldn't account for the hideous transformation of so exquisite a beauty into this…this…*hag*..

His mouth tightened. He remembered what the social worker had told him.

Drugs. Was that what had turned Rhianna Davies from a sexual temptress into this wasted, bone-thin hag?

The cruel word stabbed at him. The woman looked so terrible it would be inhuman not to feel pity for her. Yet pity was the last thing she deserved. The very last thing…

He felt the rage well up in his throat again, as it had ever since he'd looked down into the stricken face of his son.

Any child, *any,* deserved a mother better than this! On top of everything that he already knew her to be—the kind of slut who traded her body for financial gain—yet she was worse still. Irresponsible, feckless, leaving a four-year-old on his own while she slept off her despicable addiction—an addiction that made her violent, brandishing a knife at the very woman appointed to protect her child…

And that such a female was mother to *his* son! A son she had deliberately, calculatingly hidden from him, kept him ignorant of! *Thee mou,* no torment was good enough for such a woman!

And yet rigid self-control sliced down over his seething emotions. He was going to have to treat her with kid gloves. His lawyers had been blunt, even though he had wanted to hurl them from his office. The fathers of illegitimate children in the United Kingdom had no automatic right of custody. To gain custody of his son would be a complicated, controversial business. And while it was conducted his son would remain in care, certainly until his mother was physically fit enough to look after him, and possibly—if the social worker's case for wanting a Care Order were valid—indefinitely.

His jaw tightened. No—that was one thing that would *not* continue! His son was coming out of that foster woman's house—his unhappiness, his misery had been palpable.

Whatever it took—he would get his son out of there!

Even if it meant dealing sweetly with someone as contemptible as Rhianna Davies.

Alexis's eyes swept over the gaunt, haggard face staring horrified up at him. His stomach clenched. Rhianna Davies might be mercenary, an irresponsible drug-addict, but his son had cried for her...

Piercing like a needle into his memory, he heard the pinched little voice whispering, almost inaudibly, at his oh-so-carefully phrased question this morning, 'Mummy...I want Mummy.'

His nails dug into his palms. Dear God—a child crying for his mother...

A mother who never came back...

Memory gutted through him, drenching him with remembered pain, making him hear the heartbroken crying of a child for its mother. With a wrench he silenced the voice he could still hear inside his head, as if it were yesterday, not thirty long years ago.

No. Enough memories. They were no use now.

All that was needed now was his most honed negotiation skill. Rhianna Davies held the key to his son—he had to find a way to turn it. And his emotions—seething, swirling like a black inky pit inside him—were only going to get in the way of doing so. Ruthlessly, he schooled himself. Time for finesse now, not the indulgence of emotion.

Regaining control, he let his eyes rest on her appalled expression. He brought to the forefront of his mind what he had concluded her long-term plan was to be. Obviously

Rhianna Davies had kept his son from him quite deliberately, so she must have been biding her time, planning on producing him at a time of her choosing, when she would gain the greatest advantage from the disclosure.

That she had not done so as soon as she'd known she was pregnant could only have been because she had not, at that stage, been sure of his paternity. A woman as free with her favours as he knew her to be could easily have had any number of contenders for the privilege of impregnating her. Perhaps she had not been sure enough of his contribution to risk challenging him with a DNA test. Better, she must have reasoned, for her to have waited until the boy had grown sufficiently for his Greek heritage to be visible in his features. Then she would be on much safer ground to claim him as her child's father.

Well, fate had taken a hand, and disclosure had come prematurely. From his point of view that could only be a good thing. She had lost the advantage of timing. Indeed—his eyes swept over her haggard features once more—she had lost a lot more advantages as well.

Her beauty, for one.

Grimly, he could only be glad of it. Rhianna Davies's beauty had made him lose his self-control, had caused an indulgence he should *never* have allowed himself. But he was safe from her wiles now, all right. The gaunt death's head staring up at him held no allure for him—or any male.

Except—and the thought stabbed at him—a heartbroken little boy, with nothing left to cling on to but his battered teddy bear...

He took a sharp, inward breath and opened negotiations.

The most critical of his life.

He was playing for his son—and he *had* to win.

Rhianna stared. It was a vision, a nightmare—it had to be. It had to be! Alexis Petrakis was gone—gone for ever! Thrust into the oblivion of the past, nailed down in a box with the key buried so deep she would *never* open it again! For five long, gruelling years she had kept it buried—had had so much else to worry about, agonise about, exhaust herself with, that it had been all but obliterated from her mind.

Self-preservation had helped her keep the past buried, unremembered. Because to remember Alexis Petrakis would have been to remember everything he had done to her—everything she had allowed him to do.

Everything he had said to her on that hideous, hideous morning.

She had crawled away from his hotel suite shaking with shame, with revulsion at herself—at him—wanting only to hide for ever.

Instead she'd had to go back, face her father, tell him...tell him she had failed. Failed to save his company, the one thing in his life he loved above all else, far more than his discarded wife and daughter—because how could a mere family compare with his obsession to design yachts?

If I had managed to save his company...

The old, familiar taunting scraped at her. If she had been able to do the one thing that her father had craved, *needed* above all else...

Oh, then he would have loved her! Surely then he would have loved her?

But she had failed. That vile, hideous night had seen to that, had destroyed both her self-respect and her last hope of salvaging her father's company and so saving him from dwindling down through his remaining years, stricken by stroke, bereft of the one thing that had given his life meaning, increasingly ill, increasingly cantankerous, increasingly difficult to look after. Blaming her for not being the son he had wanted her to be, who would have been useful to him—not a useless girl, unable even to save his company, and now, worst of all, saddled with a fatherless bastard baby...

And all the time, like some grinding, relentless mill of God, their new poverty had crushed them exceeding fine, until they'd been reduced to living in a council flat on a sink estate that no one else wanted to live on and she had become carer to both her infant son and her invalid father, eking out their existence on state benefit.

Until the bitter, painful end had come to her father's life, draining the very last of her worn, exhausted energies…

Tiredness sapped her. She lay there now, in her hospital bed, and despair swept over her.

After all she had gone through in the last five years, now was the worst of all. Nicky—gone.

There Alexis stood, once more dominating her vision, obliterating the rest of the world for her! Once more an over-poweringly tangible and oppressive presence. Taller, it seemed than she remembered, and darker-hued. His Mediterranean origins were obvious—not just in his colour-ing, but in his stance. And, most vivid of all, the arrogance, that dominance of the Mediterranean male. Exacerbated a thousand times by the knowledge of his wealth, his power.

Power.

That was what Alexis Petrakis radiated.

Fear froze through her.

Why was he here? How was he here?

And worst of all—most terrifying of all—what did he want?

Out of nowhere the answer iced through her.

Nicky.

Fear bit like a wolf at her heart. No! He couldn't know about Nicky! He couldn't!

Sanity fought its way through her terror. Even if Alexis Petrakis *had* found out about Nicky, the last thing he'd do would be to *care* about him!

Unless it were to ensure her silence about him. To tell her not to even think of wanting financial support. But she had never, ever thought to do that! Alexis Petrakis was the last man on earth she wanted her or Nicky to have anything to do with.

So what was he doing here now?

Dread filled her.

For one long, last moment Alexis stood looking down at the haggard woman lying there. He'd had her moved to a private ward—not for her sake, but for his. Not only did he not want to talk to her in a public ward, but in a private ward he could ensure she had no access to a phone. She wouldn't be phoning the tabloid press with some scandalous story of a Greek tycoon's illegitimate son living in a council flat, with his drug addict mother!

He wondered, coldly, how she was going to play it. She was, as he knew to his cost from five years ago, a superb actress.

But he'd taken her by surprise; that was obvious from her stunned reaction. She looked terrified—and well she might.

Rage spurted through him again, and he crushed it back.

She stared at him, face stricken, features twisting.

'Why are you here?' Her voice was thin, strained. He could hear the tension in it. Inside him, the emotions he was holding back, leashed so tight it was taking him more effort than he'd thought possible to keep them in check, were nipping and snarling at him like a pack of caged wolves.

'You don't know?'

Her face tightened, with a wary expression in her eyes he did not miss. She was recovering her guard.

'How should I?'

Her evasiveness enraged him. She *dared* lie there and try and play games with him while his son was abandoned to foster care?

He subdued his rage again.

Instead, he simply said a single word.

'Nicky.'

The name fell into the silence. Into the yawning space between them.

He watched her face as he said his son's name.

It froze.

Completely.

His veiled eyes went on looking down at her expression-lessly. Dismay was etched visibly through her every haggard feature. Anger bit at him again. So he'd been right—she hadn't wanted him to know yet, had wanted to go on biding her time, keeping his son from him until she could get the best deal on him.

The best price for him.

Black fury convulsed through him. He thrust it aside. It would not help now.

Instead, he watched her, like a fly trapped in treacle, as he forced his knowledge upon her. Beneath his rigidly schooled expression he could feel his anger, leashed on a hard, tight wire.

Rhianna could only stare sickly, frozen, the air solidifying in her lungs. She couldn't move, couldn't breathe.

Oh God, he knew about Nicky...

He *knew.*

She could feel panic start to rise in her breast like a claw-ing beast.

How—*how* had he found out?

She must have mouthed the word, because his brows sud-denly drew together. For an instant, no more, there was a flash deep in his eyes. But when he spoke the tight mesh of control was still in place, draining all emotion from his voice.

But the very lack of emotion filled Rhianna with dread.

'How? Your social worker phoned me.' He paused infin-itesimally, his eyes boring down into Rhianna's. Hers were still glazed with shock, her face frozen. He went on, biting out each word, his eyes never leaving hers. 'She made very free with her views on men who fathered children and then declined to shoulder financial responsibility for them.' His voice chilled. 'She was particularly incensed that a man with my "extensive financial resources", as she phrased it, should have so evaded his obligations.' As he finished, there was ice in every word. 'She gave me to understand that she was sure I would find it both socially and reputationally embarrassing if my…neglect…of my responsibilities were to reach the courts or the press.'

Oh, God, thought Rhianna, realisation hollowing her out. So that's why he's here. That social worker has ripped into him and threatened him with the tabloids!

Her nails clenched into her palms, digging painfully. She was reeling, punch-drunk. Her mind had gone numb, completely numb. All she could feel was the horror ballooning inside her that Alexis Petrakis knew about Nicky's existence.

He was speaking again, and she tried to make sense of the words, desperately trying to pull her mind together, still reeling from shock and dismay. His clipped, staccato words cut through her flailing emotions.

'I want him out of care. Immediately.'

The hard, expressionless eyes bored down on her, drilling into her. Yes, she thought—fighting to make sense of this nightmare that had just walked through the door and seized her by the throat until she couldn't breathe, couldn't think— that's why he's here. The tabloids would have a field-day— a multimillionaire refusing to pay maintenance for his son in state foster care!

He would never risk that. And that was why he was here— to neutralise the danger to himself.

'They won't release him until I'm discharged from hospital.'

Her voice was thin. Flat. Not revealing her agony at being parted from Nicky, her gut-churning fear that he would never be returned to her. Every instinct told her to hide her emotions from this man, whose sole concern was protecting himself from scandal.

Alexis's mouth tightened. No sign of admitting that her drug addiction was keeping her son in care as much as her injuries. Let alone any sign of emotion at losing her own child! Yet again he banked down the anger roiling inside him. Time enough to throw at her head her total moral unfitness to take care of a child!

Right now, all that was important was getting Nicky out of care.

'That is no longer a problem. I have spoken to your physician and he has agreed to discharge you.'

For a second he thought he saw her eyes blaze with emotion. Then, instantly, they were blank again.

'I—I don't understand.'

His voice was terse as he spoke. 'I have informed him that I will provide appropriate nursing care for you, which means that you no longer need to be hospitalised. I have also informed the council authorities that I will provide a qualified nanny to undertake childcare. This has satisfied them to the extent that they have agreed to rescind the temporary Care Order.'

Like a vast, welling wave Rhianna felt emotion pour through her. Oh, God, did this really, really mean she could get Nicky back? Hope soared within her. Though she would rather eat dirt than let Alexis Petrakis anywhere near her and Nicky, if he was the only way of getting Nicky back then she would do it.

But she must not, must *not* let him see how much it meant to her. God, did she not know how ruthless he was? How vile? He was already clearly furious that his hand had been forced like this—a bastard son who threatened his reputation foisted on him.

She looked up at the hard, shuttered face of the man who had once turned her insides to mush, who had been able to seduce her as effortlessly as taking candy from a baby. It had been the most incredible night of her life, but in the morning—

Her mind sheered away.

Nicky—her beloved son. He was all that was important now. And she must not show her desperation to get him back.

She forced a cool, unnatural calmness into her voice.

'So what happens next?'

Alexis's pupils narrowed. A stab of cold rage bit at him. *Christos,* her cold-blooded reaction damned her! Like a snake deep in a pit, memory writhed within him, struggling to be let out, to be remembered... He thrust it back. Only one thing now was important—his son. When he spoke, his voice was as impassive as before.

'You will be discharged tomorrow, into the care of the nurse I have hired. Together with the nanny, your car will call at the foster home *en route* to the airport—'

'What do you mean, airport?' Rhianna's interjection was sharp, high-pitched. Every aching muscle in her battered body tensed, alarm bells shrieking.

Alexis Petrakis looked down at her without expression. 'You will be flying to Greece—'

'*Greece?*'

Dark eyes flickered coldly.

'You will stay in my villa, by the sea. It is on a private island that I own. It is very luxurious, fully staffed. You will be waited on hand and foot.'

With a slow, painful exhalation Rhianna understood. Her battered mind had fastened on to the single phrase that made sense to her. 'Private island' he had said.

So that was what this was about—he was going to hide her and Nicky away on his private island, safe from prying eyes. For him, it made sense. But for her and Nicky?

How could she possibly let herself and Nicky be taken to Greece by Alexis Petrakis? Locked away on a private island, surrounded by Petrakis staff!

But it was the only way she could get Nicky out of care.

And that was all, *all* that was important.

It didn't matter how she got him back! Didn't matter that the man she hated more than anyone else in the world was doing it for his own selfish, self-protecting reasons. It only mattered that Alexis Petrakis was using his wealth and position to make state bureaucracy, the medical system, work in his favour.

Besides—another thought came into her reeling, over-wrought mind—a villa by the sea. Alexis Petrakis had thrown that at her.

A beach…

The seaside…

It would be like a holiday for Nicky. A holiday after the trauma of being taken from her.

He'd never been on holiday…

Her thoughts flew on.

It would be warmer in Greece, too, and with a nurse for her and a nanny to help with Nicky she could get well faster there—much faster than in the bleak, damp flat she lived in. And once she was well she could get Nicky back properly again, without having to rely on Alexis Petrakis's wealth.

And then—her mouth tightened—then Alexis Petrakis could go to hell.

CHAPTER FOUR

ALEXIS threw himself into the back of his car, silent rage consuming him. He could feel it streaming through him like a dark flowing river. Rage that for four silent, invisible years his son had lived and breathed and he had known nothing, *nothing* of his existence! That drugged-out woman had kept him from him, hidden him away until the time was ripe for her to cash in on him...cash in on her own son!

He felt his hands clench, and he had to force himself to unclench them. On the other side of town his son was sitting huddled in a chair, 'failing to thrive' as the social worker had acidly informed him.

His hands clenched again and rage surged once more.

It would be spent, he knew, only when he had his son in his possession.

Safe.

Carefully, the hospital porter pushed Rhianna's wheelchair up the ramp into the waiting limo. Two women got into the car after her—one middle-aged in a nurse's uniform, the other younger than her, with a cheerful face. They smiled at Rhianna, introducing themselves, but she hardly paid attention.

Her heart was hammering in her breast, adrenaline running, bringing with it fear and desperate hope. Her mouth was dry, her throat tight as a drum. Her nails bit into her palms, lying on her lap swathed in a rug.

Nicky, Nicky, Nicky...

Like a litany, her son's name went round and round in her head.

The limo moved off. Smooth though the ride was, every

stop and start in the traffic seemed to jar right through her. Her breathing was slow and laboured, her punished lungs still weak. Her bruised and battered body still fragile.

But she didn't care. She could have ached a thousand times worse and she would not have cared—so long as she was going to where Nicky was…

How long the journey took she had no idea. Her hands were clasped tight into one another, twisting and clenching as she stared blindly out ahead through the windscreen. The weather was bleak, with a lowering sky. Spring seemed a million miles away.

The limo glided to a halt along the kerb of a busy arterial road lined with pre-war semis. They stopped by one with a small ironwork gate and a concrete path leading to the front door. The nurse and nanny climbed out. Rhianna strained forward, trying to see out of the open car door towards the house.

She did not see the sleek silver chauffeured saloon car draw up behind the limo, nor the tall, dark-suited figure climb out, and stand, his face drawn, looking up at the nondescript house. The front door opened and a woman came out.

Alexis watched the scene silently. He recognised the foster carer, still with a toddler fastened to her hip. She was talking to a woman beside her—neither the nurse nor the nanny, both of whom were still in the porch of the house. The other woman nodded, her face tight, and then reached out her hand peremptorily before starting to walk forward along the path. Her gait was slower than an adult's, and Alexis felt his stomach clench as he realised she was leading forward a small, diminutive figure whose hunched frame and bowed head made his throat tighten. Her other hand carried a suitcase. The nurse and nanny fell into step, the nurse starting to talk to the third woman, who talked back to her, her face still set in lines of disapproval. Instinctively, emotion impelling him, he started to move forwards, towards the diminutive, hunched figure.

And then suddenly, there was a cry. A cry so high, so thin, Alexis's head jerked round.

'Nicky!'

It was a cry that was half a sob. At the sound of it the bowed, dragging figure looked up, eyes huge in his little face. And then, like an instant tornado, he tore down the concrete path, across the pavement, and threw himself into the car.

'Mummy! Mummy! Mummy! Mummy!'

The piping voice was shrill, hysterical. Rhianna bent and scooped him onto her lap, clutching him to her, oblivious of the physical pain in her chest, lost in the joy that overwhelmed her. Tears poured down her face.

'Oh, Nicky—Nicky!' She crushed him against her, tears choking in her throat, ecstasy in her heart. 'Oh, my darling, my darling! Mummy's own best boy!'

Sobs were racking through her, and she thought she must die of happiness as she held the son she had never thought to see again safe in her arms.

Outside on the pavement Alexis Petrakis stood, immobile, watching.

His face was set like stone.

The car was moving again. Rhianna was oblivious to it—oblivious to everything except the little hand clutching hers so tightly it wrung her heart.

'Have you been a good boy, my darling?' she asked Nicky, her hand cupping his cheek. He was as close as possible to the wheelchair, fastened safely into a child seat that had materialised from nowhere.

He nodded, his eyes huge.

'You weren't there,' he said.

'Your mummy's been ill, poppet,' the nanny chipped in. She was sitting next to Nicky, while the nurse sat on a fold-down seat opposite.

'But I'm getting better,' Rhianna added hurriedly.

'Are we going home now?' Nicky asked. There was a painful eagerness in his little voice that stabbed at her.

She started to speak, but the nurse got in first.

'Your mother isn't well enough to look after you all on your own yet, young man,' she said in a firm voice. 'So she's going to have a little holiday—yes, *with* you. Don't worry! Mr Petrakis has it all arranged.'

Nicky's eyes widened.

'A holiday? Mummy! Are we? Where?'

There was anxiety underlying the astonishment, she could hear. He'd been through so much. She couldn't bear it if he was to be upset now when he discovered they were not just going home after all. It might just be a run-down council flat, but it was the only home he could remember. She swallowed and made herself smile. *Please* let him be OK with what was going to happen to them. She injected enthusiasm into her voice.

'Far away! It's an adventure! We're going in an aeroplane.'

Nicky's mouth opened in disbelief.

'An *airyplane*?' he echoed, in an awed voice.

'Yes,' she answered, filled with relief that he was not upset about not going back to his familiar home. 'An airyplane.'

She squeezed Nicky's tightly clutching hand and felt tears of joy seep into her eyes.

She had got Nicky back. Her precious son.

She would never let him go ever again. No matter the cost to herself.

Seven hours later Rhianna felt as if she'd been hit by a speeding car all over again. Every bone in her body ached, it seemed, and her lungs were like a soggy swamp. Even with luxury travel—a private executive jet from the local city airport, a helicopter from Athens to Alexis Petrakis's private island in the Aegean, a stretcher to convey her to a bedroom in his villa—she was still exhausted.

It made her realise how impossible it would have been to look after Nicky at home on her own.

Conducted by a large black-clothed woman, who spoke

English with a strong Greek accent and who introduced herself as Maria, Karen, the nanny, took Nicky off to his bedroom, in between hers and his mother's, while Nurse Thompson got her patient into bed.

Rhianna's last waking sight, some little while later, before she gave herself up to the cool, crisp sheets and the soft, soft pillows, was Nicky, padding into her room in his worn pyjamas, clutching his faithful teddy, and Karen lifting him carefully onto her bed so that he could kiss her goodnight.

'Sleep tight, Mummy,' he said, and wrapped his little arms around her neck to kiss her. 'Don't ever go away again.'

Bliss washed through her.

'My darling—never,' she murmured, and slid away to sleep the sleep of angels in paradise.

Alexis gave her a week.

It was longer by seven days than he'd wanted it to be. With every instinct he possessed he wanted to be with his son. To start making up—*now*—for the four years without him.

But the relationship that he was going to start now—four years late—was going to have to last a lifetime. He had to get it right. *Thee mou,* he knew what happened when a father failed to get it right...

It was also seven days longer than he'd wanted to leave it before he saw Rhianna Davies again. Not that his desire to set eyes on her again was driven by anything like the same instinct that was impelling him to his son.

The opposite entirely.

How strange, he thought, with a hardening of his eyes as he sat staring into the middle distance from behind his desk in his corporate HQ in Athens, that he could love his son so much—and hate the mother.

Deliberately he made himself relax the tensed muscles in his back and shoulders. Rhianna Davies was no longer an issue. She existed now for one purpose only—to be there if his son wanted her. For his son's sake alone he would tolerate her existence. It might gall him to know he had to finance her in a life of ease simply because she was the mother of his son, but by the same token it was the way he was going to be able to control her. She would remain there, for his son, or he would let her drop back into the gutter. He would make it very, very clear on what terms he would tolerate her existence in his son's life.

A frown flickered across his brow. One thing, however, he would not tolerate. The drugs had to go. However long it took to get her off them, go they must. A look of disgust fleeted in his eyes. God knew, he didn't expect much from a woman of her stamp—amoral and venal—but surely the mirror alone should have told her what drugs were doing to her? They'd sucked the beauty from her as surely as they'd sucked her health! The image of her gaunt death's head intruded in his mind, and then an image from the night she'd come to him, five years ago. The contrast was grotesque, repulsive.

He thrust both images from him and reached for his phone. His schedule this week had been more punishing than anything he'd ever put himself through. In a single week he had cleared out of the way everything that needed to be dealt with at Petrakis International. Once he reached the villa he wanted nothing to make him leave again for at least a month. His pilot could bring him any documents he needed, and his study there was equipped with communications to the rest of his empire.

Not that he wanted work to distract him. His entire focus was going to be on his son—the son who did not yet even know that he was his father.

Acid anger seethed again in his guts like sour bile.

Rhianna sat back in the padded reclining chair and gazed out over the scene ahead of her. A profound and heartfelt wash of happiness and gratitude swept through her. All around her the gentle warmth of the Mediterranean spring lapped like swansdown. A soft golden sun, radiant in the late-afternoon sky, was blessing down upon the white-flecked blue of the sea curved into the little bay. From the vine-shaded, stone-paved terrace on which her chair was positioned she could easily see over the balustrade on to the sandy beach, a mere eight feet below. Nicky, in T-shirt, shorts and sun hat, was down there, contentedly digging in the sand by the seashore, with Karen to look after him.

With a child's resilience, safe and secure again with his mother there, and all the happiness of a small child by the seaside, Nicky already seemed to be over the trauma of having being separated from his mother. As for herself, she was feeling so much better too. Now that her anxiety was gone, her body was free to get on with the task of healing itself— a task made so much easier in the balmy warmth of the Aegean in this luxurious villa, with the ministrations of Nurse Thompson and the complete absence of any housework and childcare.

It was certainly a blissful way to live.

For a moment she felt a stab of guilt go through her. Had she not kept Nicky's existence from Alexis Petrakis her son might have grown up in surroundings like this. However grudgingly he'd have done it, the state authorities would have required him to take financial responsibility for his offspring, however unintended.

Her expression hardened.

No—not in exchange for all the financial support in the world would she ever have told Alexis Petrakis about Nicky! Some fathers were just not worth having. Hadn't her own sorry childhood taught her that? With her mother constantly hoping that her errant husband would return, and herself yearning for a father who had no interest in her. No—better for Nicky to have no father than one who was worse than nothing, a father he might spend his life trying to get to love him in vain...

The way she had.

A growing noise cut off her thoughts. Down on the beach she saw Nicky and Karen crane their necks upwards. A moment later Rhianna realised what it was. A helicopter, getting closer, the racket from its rotors deafening her as it started to descend.

Was it the doctor again? she wondered. He'd been out twice to see her—firstly on the day after she'd arrived, and then the day before yesterday. But he'd been pleased with her progress and wasn't due again till next week.

So who could this be? Arriving now, like this?

She did not have long to wait to find out.

Alexis's mouth tightened as he strode out on to the terrace. Surprise was always a reliable element of attack. Had she really thought she would be allowed to settle down here, in the lap of luxury, and not be called to account?

Then his eyes slid past her, out down on to the beach, and he stilled.

His son was paddling in the sea, laughing and splashing, jumping up and down over the tiny waves with glee.

Alexis heart constricted.

It was a totally different child from the one he'd seen with the foster carer, withdrawn and traumatised.

Again, that overpowering emotion poured through him— a fierce, consuming protectiveness.

'What are you doing here?'

The thin, high-pitched voice cut through his emotion.

He turned his head sharply, eyes turning cold. They locked on to the woman who had given birth to his son, then kept him from him for four long years.

She had gone stark white, her pallor emphasising the hollowness of her cheeks, the deep circles around her sunken eyes. Shock was etched through every line.

'What are you doing here?' she demanded again, in the same constricted voice.

He lowered himself into one of the rattan chairs. For a moment he said nothing, just studied her. As if she were some kind of cockroach. She was still looking shell-shocked.

There were other emotions in her face, but he didn't have time to waste identifying them.

'We have matters to…discuss.'

She knew then just why he had come. There could be on only one reason.

'You want me to sign papers, don't you? Legally preventing me from ever going to the press about Nicky.'

Despite the shock thudding through her, she fought to keep her voice unshaky.

Alexis's dark, damning eyes hardened. So that was to have been her plan, was it? Threatening to expose his son in the gutter press for all the world to gawp at!

With deliberate slowness, to give himself time to still the stab of fury that her words had catalysed, he sat back.

'You will never,' he informed her, 'speak to the press about my son. With or without any legal binding. Why do you imagine I brought you here? For the sake of your health?' The irony in his tone was scathing.

'And when I take Nicky back to England?' she retorted. He was bound to want some kind of legally enforceable silencing of her—but she didn't care. She'd sign anything he wanted just to get rid of him as fast as possible. Preferably right now.

'You will not be returning to England—and nor will my son.'

There was no emotion audible in his voice. Not a trace of it. It was like cold steel going into her.

'From now on,' he went on, in the same tone, 'you will be living here. Later, when he is school age and fluent in Greek, other arrangements will be made.'

'*School* age? Fluent in Greek? What the *hell* are you talking about?'

Dark, dead eyes rested on her.

'I am talking about the way my son will live now.'

Rhianna's mouth flattened to a tight line.

'Hand me the papers to sign, Mr Petrakis! It's a lot simpler than the idiocy you're proposing as an alternative!'

It seemed to her that the dark eyes went even more dead.

'You don't get a choice. My son stays in Greece. And while, as a child, he has *any* need of you, you stay too. This is non-negotiable.'

She stared—just stared.

'You're insane. Do you really imagine that I'm going to stay incarcerated here just for *your* sake?'

In the depths of his unblinking eyes there was a sudden dark flash.

'What I "really imagine" is that from now on you will do *exactly* as I tell you! Understand this and understand it well! You have *no* negotiating power!'

She jerked forward in her seat. It hurt her ribs but she didn't care. Disbelief and anger were boiling through her.

'I wouldn't negotiate with you if my life depended on it!'

'That is as well.' The retort was flat. 'You are beginning—finally—to understand your situation.'

Rhianna's heart started to pound, heavy and thudding. Alexis Petrakis was speaking again. His voice was cold. Deadly. His eyes were as hard as obsidian.

'Let me spell out your situation to you—so that even you can understand it. Whatever fond dreams you have been entertaining that I will set you up in luxury in England, content merely to see my son as a visitor, you may now set them aside. My son will be a permanent part of my life from now on. You will live here, under supervision, while I seek to rectify the damage you have done to my son by keeping him from me. I have lost four years—*four years*—of his life, and I should destroy you for that. But my hands are tied—while he is a child my son's happiness is dependent on you, and for that reason alone I tolerate your presence in his life. Have absolutely no doubts about that.'

She felt nothing—nothing at all. Only drowning, disbelieving horror. She could not, could *not* have heard him say what he had just said!

'And now—' his voice bit, dark, killing fire scorching in

his eyes '—I will start undoing four years of my son not knowing of my existence!'

She wanted to scream, to shout, but she could not. She was frozen—frozen with horror.

He was walking down the stone steps to the beach, moving lithely in his lightweight suit. It should have looked incongruous, walking across a beach with a hand-tailored business suit on, but it only reinforced his power.

Where she found the strength she did not know. But pressing down on the chair's arms, she levered herself up, feeling the world wheel round her. She didn't care. She staggered towards the steps, sick and faint. She could see Nicky, still splashing in the shallow water, happy and playful, while towards him walked a man who, if she could have, right now she would have obliterated on the spot.

She clutched at the stone balustrade at the edge of the steps, forcing her legs to work though her heart was pounding in terror. She opened her mouth to scream, to yell a warning, a negation, an utter negation of what was happening, but instead there was a black mist rolling in, like a diesel train rushing up to her. Her legs collapsed and suddenly she was pitched head forward into total darkness.

Alexis heard the thud of her body collapsing on the sand and wheeled round. Simultaneously he heard a gasp of shock from the nanny sitting on the towel, who had already started to get to her feet at his approach. Her eyes flew past him to Rhianna's huddled form.

'Look after Nicky!' bit out Alexis, and strode back towards the villa. 'Keep him away!'

She was out cold. With a sharp voice he called out for the nurse, then scooped the inert body up into his arms. She weighed hardly anything—but she was a dead weight for all that. He hurried up the steps with her and took her inside.

The nurse was hurrying towards him, exclaiming, but he silenced her.

'Which bedroom does she have?'

'In here,' the woman replied, and opened the door to the master bedroom, which opened up onto its own section of the terrace around the corner from the beach terrace.

Ungently, Alexis deposited his burden on the bed. 'She tried to get down the steps and collapsed on the sand.' He answered the nurse's brisk enquiry tersely. At least the woman seemed competent enough not to make a fuss. She was checking pulse and heart, straightening her patient's body.

'Do you need to call a doctor?' Alexis demanded.

The nurse looked up briefly and shook her head. 'She'll come to in a moment,' she predicted, and returned her attention to her patient.

Alexis nodded, mouth tight. He left her to it and went outdoors again. On the beach he could see the nanny, crouching down beside Nicky, talking to him and clearly holding him back from rushing inside. Alexis felt another spurt of anger. Had Rhianna no sense at all? Frightening the boy like that? Or had she done it deliberately? His brow darkened. What was she trying now? Another affecting little scene like the one she'd put on for him when the boy had come out of care? Fawning all over him to prove how maternal she was suddenly?

Just like his own mother—

No. No memories. None. He would not allow it.

He slammed his mind shut.

Calming himself deliberately, he walked down to the beach and up to his son. Rhianna Davies was nothing to him. His son was everything.

As he approached he felt his emotions start to churn again, but he suppressed them. To the child he was a stranger. He must not forget that. And right now the boy's main concern was his mother, after seeing her collapse like that. Fear was naked on his little face.

Alexis took a breath, forcing his voice to sound reassuring.

'It is nothing to worry about,' he said. He looked at the boy, dragging on his nanny's hand. 'Your mother will be better in a moment. Nurse Thompson is with her. She just felt dizzy.'

The nanny took up the cue. 'Giddy—that's all! Your mummy has to take it easy, remember? She's been ill, but she's getting better. Now, look—you've got a visitor! Mr Petrakis?'

She straightened up and looked at Alexis. She was very good, he registered. Professional. Whether she had guessed his relationship to her charge or not he neither knew nor cared. He gave her a brief, dismissing nod and she took her cue again, saying brightly, 'Goodness me, look at the mess! Time for me to tidy everything up!' She headed back to the mound of beach toys, and started gathering them into a pile. Alexis watched his son look uncertainly from his nanny to him.

His nanny of one week was more familiar to him than his own father.

I'm a stranger. A complete stranger to him.
Thanks to his mother. Keeping him from me.
Bitterness seared through him.

And much more—a rush of fierce emotion. This would be the last time in his life when he would be a stranger to his own son. Starting now.

Carefully, very carefully, he took the first step on that crucial journey.

'Hello, Nicky. Have you been having fun playing on the beach?'

For a moment Nicky's expression wavered. Then it brightened.

'I've been in the sea!' he announced.

With his heart still tight in his chest, Alexis made himself smile. It seemed hard to make the muscles around his mouth do that. He wondered, offhand, when he'd last smiled. Not since Maureen Carter had put the call through from the social worker, that was for sure.

'Have you? What did you do in the sea?'

The big eyes shone.

'Splashing!'

'Show me.'

There was no hesitation. His son filled up his bucket and then ejected the contents seawards.

'See?' He twisted his head round to Alexis.

'Very good. Which do you think goes further? A bucket of water or a stone?'

He watched as his son put down the bucket and picked up a small pebble.

'Stone!' shouted Nicky, as it plonked into the water, further out to sea.

He picked up another one and threw it.

'I know a trick with stones,' said Alexis. He walked forward, almost to the sea's edge. A quick, crouching search in the sand revealed a couple of round, flat pebbles. He straightened, hoping he could still do what he'd promised. He looked out to sea, narrowing his eyes with concentration as he readied his aim and the angle of his throw.

'It bounced!' His son's voice was amazed. He looked up at Alexis, astonishment and respect in his face. 'Do it again!'

Alexis obliged.

'*Two* bounces!' shouted Nicky. He jumped up and down. The water splashed Alexis's trouser leg. He couldn't care less.

'Make it *three!*' ordered Nicky.

'Next time,' said Alexis. He knew when to quit. He was amazed himself that he could still do that with flat pebbles. Memory stabbed through him. He'd taught himself how to do it as a boy, with painstaking, dogged, untaught practice during the endless summers he'd spent by the sea in the huge Petrakis summer villa on the coast of Attica. There'd never been anyone to play with. His father had always stayed in Athens, working.

As for his mother—

He sliced down the steel door, shutting out the past.

His son was picking up stones and trying to make them bounce, without success.

'I can't do it!' His voice was frustrated.

'It's a trick. I told you. I'll teach you, but when you're older.'

'When I'm five?' said Nicky.

'Older. I learnt the trick when I was older than five.'

'How old?'

Alexis thought back. He didn't want to, but he found himself doing it anyway.

'Eight,' he announced.

Exactly eight, he remembered. It had been his birthday. His father had been in New York, on business. Alexis had been in the villa on his own, apart from the staff. He'd spent the day on the beach, doggedly practising with stones until he could make them bounce.

'I will be eight in...' His son carefully counted on his fingers, bringing Alexis back to the present, shutting the past back into its bleak grave. 'One, two, three, *four* years.'

'Very good,' said Alexis. '*Kala.* That means good in Greek.' He paused. 'We are in Greece. This is one of the Greek islands. There are hundreds of islands in Greece. If you can count in English,' he went on, 'you can count in Greek. *Ena, thio, tria.* That's one, two, three. Can you say that?'

Hesitantly, the little boy repeated the numbers. Something pierced inside Alexis.

My son. Speaking Greek to me.

'Very good,' he said, and smiled down at his son.

It seemed easier, that second smile.

CHAPTER FIVE

RHIANNA stirred, sluggishly. Her head felt heavy; her body was aching. She must have been given a sedative, and the after-effects had made her feel groggy. She wondered how long she'd been asleep, and reached for her watch. As she did so she realised she was wearing her nightdress. Nurse Thompson must have got her changed, though she did not remember it.

The watch showed ten-thirty a.m., and she realised she had slept through till morning.

Simultaneously she remembered just *why* Nurse Thompson must have sedated her.

Panic leapt in her breast.

'Nicky!'

Her voice was anguished.

Had she called out loud?

An instant later Nurse Thompson was entering her bedroom.

'Now, now,' she said calmly. 'I will not have you upsetting yourself again—'

'Where's Nicky?' Rhianna demanded desperately. Fear filled her. Cold, terrifying fear.

Nurse Thompson answered composedly. 'He's swimming in the pool with Mr Petrakis.'

Immediately Rhianna tried to throw off her bedclothes. Nurse Thompson pressed her back.

'This won't do,' she said sternly. 'Nicky is perfectly all right, and perfectly happy. You can see him in just a little while, when you've had breakfast. He isn't going anywhere.'

But Rhianna only stared up at her with anguished eyes.

'You don't understand—'

Nurse Thompson plumped her pillows.

'What I understand is this: if you want to get well, as fast as possible, you simply must not upset yourself like this! You could have fallen quite badly on those steps yesterday, you know. And what help would that have been? Now, eat your breakfast, and then I'll help you get up.'

There was nothing Rhianna could do but give in. But even as she forced down her breakfast under the unyielding supervision of Nurse Thompson her head was going round and round.

Desperately she tried to force her brain to think, to function. Alexis Petrakis could not take Nicky from her. The fathers of illegitimate children had no automatic rights in law. She could deny him access, keep Nicky safe from him, get a family court to keep Alexis Petrakis away...

But even as her thoughts writhed like snakes a question kept stabbing through her that she could not, *could not* answer.

Why? *Why* did Alexis Petrakis want Nicky? Surely the only reason he'd got him out of foster care and brought him here with her was to stop any scandal breaking?

But why was he so angry that she had kept him from him? Emotion choked in her.

Dear God, of *course* she had kept Nicky from him! A man like that, capable of doing what he had to her, saying what he had. If he could use women like that he could do the same to his son. Her son.

It seemed an age before Nurse Thompson was finally contented by the amount she'd forced herself to eat, and helped her get dressed. Then it seemed an age to get her out on to the terrace.

'I want to be near the pool,' Rhianna said tersely. She could hear splashing, and Nicky's childish cries answered by a deeper, accented voice, coming from the direction of the lower terrace, around the other side of the villa, where the pool was.

Nurse Thompson helped her along with Stavros, Maria's husband, carrying her chair around the corner. He positioned it so that it overlooked the lower pool terrace. As the pool came into view Rhianna felt her heart crush. Nicky was there, wearing armbands, batting his way across the width. Alexis Petrakis was standing in the water, just in front of him, holding his hands out towards him, calling out encouragement.

As she watched, breath tight in her chest, Rhianna's eyes fixed on her son. But another image was burning itself on her retina. That of the man backing slowly towards the edge of the pool, his hair like wet sable, his strong, leanly muscled torso a dark, tanned gold, diamond drops of water caught in the arrow of dark hair from his pectorals to his navel.

Memory sliced like a knife through her brain. *Her hands sliding over the hard, taut cusps of his shoulders beneath the loosened lawn of his shirt, her hips straining up to his, her breath short and frantic with need, sensation pouring through her body, heat exploding through her…*

No! She must not remember! All she must do was see Alexis Petrakis now, as the man who wanted to take her son…

Emotion shuddered through her.

He would never do so. Never. No one would *ever* take Nicky away from her again. No one would *ever* part her from him.

Into her head the searing hiss of his words scalded.

My son will be a permanent part of my life from now on.

Again, disbelief knifed through her. Why, *why* did Alexis Petrakis want Nicky?

Her eyes gazed down on the scene in the pool.

'Kick!' Rhianna could hear Alexis call out. 'Kick hard!'

She watched Nicky respond by kicking even harder, propelling himself forward.

'*Kala!* Good!'

He was nodding encouragingly to Nicky, beckoning him

forwards all the time. He had eyes only for the boy. Total focus. Total attention.

It didn't make sense. It just didn't make sense.

And yet, as she went on watching, something hollowed out inside her.

Nicky was swimming towards his father. His little face rapt with concentration, with effort. With a last flurry of arms he reached him, and Alexis finally allowed his hands to be taken.

'Excellent!' he announced.

Nicky looked at him, beaming. Then he caught sight of Rhianna, watching him from the upper terrace.

'Did you see, Mummy? Did you see? I'm swimming! I'm swimming!'

His little face was a picture of delight and pleasure and pride.

Another pair of eyes rested on her. Dark, like his son's. But the look he levelled at Rhianna was black with loathing.

The morning seemed to last for ever. The swimming lesson changed into a water polo session, causing much glee for Nicky, followed by a jumping-in session which caused even more. Rhianna stared, hollow-eyed.

Watching Alexis Petrakis with her son.

When the swimming finally ended, with Karen coming out to the pool area and telling Nicky it was lunchtime, she felt that an aeon had passed.

Reluctantly, Nicky climbed out of the pool and let Karen peel his armbands off and wrap a towel round him. Rhianna could see Alexis Petrakis saying something to the nanny, and her nodding, then something to Nicky, and him saying something eagerly back. Exchange finished, Alexis Petrakis pushed off from the side of the pool and started to plough powerfully down to the deep end in a strong, rhythmic freestyle.

Nicky came racing up the steps to her.

'Did you see, Mummy? Did you see?'

He clambered up on her lap, towel and all, wet hair dripping on her. She didn't care. She just hugged him close.

Her heart clenched. *Oh, Nicky, my adored boy, I love you so much...*

'Come along—lunchtime.' Karen was holding out her hand. 'We've got to get you changed first.'

She smiled at Rhianna and led Nicky off.

Below, in the pool, Alexis Petrakis was still lapping, length after length. Sunlight rippled over the sleek shape of his body.

Rhianna's stomach churned.

Alexis lifted himself out of the pool, lithely hauling himself out by the strength of his arms alone and straightening up. He'd needed those lengths. Needed them to wash the bile from his stomach, to take the edge off his anger.

She was still sitting there, on the upper terrace. The staff had had the good sense to clear out, and that was as well. Seizing a beach towel from a pool lounger, he started to dry himself vigorously. Then, throwing the damp towel over one shoulder, he headed up the steps.

Did she stiffen as he came past her? He didn't know. He refused to look at her.

Then, as he strode past, her voice hissed at him like a venomous snake.

'You're not getting Nicky. You're not getting him.'

Alexis stopped dead. Slowly he turned to look at her.

Her hands were clenched around the arms of her chair. Her face was vehement.

His was like cold marble.

Slowly he spoke.

'Let me make something very, very plain to you.' His words were like stones. 'Any fond idea that you might now be entertaining, that you can threaten me with a custody battle that will end in your victory and a hefty maintenance payout from me, you can lose straight away. No court in Europe would give a child back to a woman like you!'

Her face contorted. 'No court in Europe would give a child to a man like *you*. They'd only have to hear how Nicky was conceived to have you thrown out of court!'

A vicious light lit his eyes. Anger lashed from him, as sharp and as violent as a knife striking.

'*Thee mou*, you have the audacity to talk about how he was conceived?'

Fury bit in her throat. Fury, and a burning shame at how easily she had fallen into Alexis Petrakis' bed. Crimson seared across her cheeks.

'I've done only one thing—*one*—that I ever regretted, and that was being so incredibly, *criminally* stupid as to fall into bed with you that night!'

Venom spat in her voice. Her heart was racing, hammering, but she had to fight back. She had to!

His mouth twisted. His eyes were killing, like a basilisk.

'Yes, stupid indeed. Stupid to take me for the fool you thought me.'

'I was not—'

But her objection was cut short by what he said next, sweeping through her hissing interjection.

'And stupid now if you think that I'd leave my son to the tender mercies of a drug addict.'

Her mouth opened, then closed again. She sat back, motionless.

'What did you say?'

Her voice was hollow.

His face was cold now, cold as the grave.

'Are you going to deny it?' His voice was vicious. 'Don't even try. The social worker who informed me I had a four-year-old son told me all about your habit. She found the evidence the morning she came to your flat and found you passed out, with spilt drugs on the bedside table and my son unattended, willing to open the door to anyone who called!

And then to take a four-year-old child out with you, when you were still high, and nearly get him killed on the road!' His eyes narrowed. 'I could throttle you for that with my bare hands, you irresponsible—'

She could feel her teeth start to chatter.

'It wasn't drugs. It was flu powder!' she interrupted.

He ignored her protestation.

'And you threatened her with violence.'

'It was a vegetable knife—I was peeling carrots! She was going on and on and on at me, badgering me to tell her who Nicky's father was—as if I would *ever* have told her that.'

'No,' he cut back at her, his voice scathing with anger, 'you wanted to plan your disclosure, didn't you? Time it for just when you could get the most money off me. And to hell with the kind of life you were subjecting my son to till you picked your moment to move in for the kill!'

Her face worked. 'You're mad. Completely insane. I was never going to let you come anywhere *near* Nicky for the rest of his life.'

Something flashed in his eyes, and she almost reeled from it. But the adrenaline was coursing through her body, making her fight, and fight, and fight.

'So that was why you ensured my name and contact details were carefully attached to his birth certificate?' His taunt was a scathing sneer.

Rhianna closed her eyes, then opened them again. Her hands were clenching in her lap.

'It was for emergencies! In case anything…anything ever happened to me.' Cold sweat ran down her back. Something very nearly *had* happened to her—if she hadn't jerked herself and the buggy away just in time as that speeding car bore down on her at the pedestrian crossing, even if Nicky had survived, she might not have. 'I put your name down because I knew that at least you had money, that the state could get you to pay out for him, pay for decent foster care…ensure a future for him…'

Again something moved in his face.

'Well, now my son *has* a future. And not with some feck-less, drugged-out—'

Rhianna clambered to her feet, ignoring the pain shooting through her as she did so.

'Don't speak to me like that! How dare you call me that? I am *not* a drug addict!'

His brows snapped together. 'Call it anything you want—recreational user—whatever obscene euphemism you want. But I tell you this, you'll never touch drugs again for the rest of your life. My son will not have an addict for a mother!'

'*I don't do drugs!*' Her voice was a high-pitched shriek. 'I have *never* done drugs!'

He looked at her coldly.

'Control yourself. I won't tolerate your hysterics. Nor will I be influenced by them.' Hard, condemning eyes bored into her. 'I know you for what you are, so don't prate to me of virtues you do not possess. Now, sit down before you fall down. And don't even think of trying to play the sympathy card. Your physical condition is entirely your own respon-sibility. My *only* concern is my son! If it weren't for him—' his eyes were a glittering mask of loathing '—you could drop dead right now and I wouldn't lift a finger to save you. But a four-year-old child needs his mother—even one such as you. So for his sake I will tolerate you and your presence in his life, but on *my* terms, do you understand me? From now on you live at my discretion, at my direction, under the su-pervision of my staff. You don't move, speak or act unless it is in the interest of my son.'

A harsh, disbelieving and derisive laugh broke from her.

'Go to hell! No court in the land will let you do that!'

He smiled. It chilled her to the bone.

'And how will you apply to the courts, I wonder? This is my island. The staff work for me, are answerable to me. Only to me.' Emotion suddenly blazed in his eyes, as if it could no longer be contained. 'My God, you *dare* to fight me? You keep my son from me for *four years* and you think I am going to be in a forgiving mood when I discover his existence? Four years of his life I've missed—all of his life he has never known what it is to have a father. Well, that ends *now!*'

She stood swaying, the world moving in and out around her.

'Why?' she whispered. 'Why are you doing this? I don't understand. What *possible* interest do you have in Nicky?'

If she had thought his face carved from stone before, now it was as if it were made of granite.

'*Thee mou*,' he said in a low voice, 'if ever you condemned yourself out of your own mouth, you have now. Now you have betrayed exactly what you are. A woman so completely bereft of humanity that you can understand *nothing* of what it means to have a child.'

There was a bleakness in his voice that seemed to drain the light from the sun. He was overwhelmed by his own scarring memories for a moment. His eyes rested on her unseeingly, then they shifted back into focus. Hard, condemning focus.

'Keep out of my sight. I don't want to breathe the same air as you.'

He walked away.

She felt faintness drumming around her, closing in on her. She clasped the stone balustrade, fighting for breath. Her heart was pounding in her chest. She could hardly breathe. The blood pressure surged in her skull. She felt sick and dizzy.

But it was not the pain in her body that was crucifying her.

'Nicky,' she whispered.

It took all Alexis's self-control to get through lunch with his son. It had been a mistake to try and eat with him. His fury was still seething through his veins, whipping him into a cold, relentless rage. He could not put it aside.

Her defiance against him enraged him. Her lies, her despicable attempts at self-exoneration, trying to whitewash her drugs habit.

The kind of woman who would try and persuade you black was white, that filthy slush was driven snow!

His memories slammed into him. His eyes grew bleak.

His mother's lovers. So many of them.

He'd even seen one of them in bed with her.

He could remember it clearly. Coming into his mother's bedroom early one morning, escaping his nurse. Clambering up onto her bed. Seeing someone else there with her. Not his father. His mother waking, seeing him, shouting angrily for his nurse, yelling at her. His nurse rushing in, scooping him away. Him starting to cry, to hang on to the blankets, which pulled back, revealing the naked sleeping form of Demos, who cleaned the pool with a strange sucking tube that used to fascinate him...

Like a guillotine he brought the blade down on the memory.

Across the table, Nicky was drinking gluggingly from a blue plastic mug adorned with the image of a cartoon character.

My son, thought Alexis, with that surge of fierce protectiveness going through him. My son.

Even if his mother is as worthless as mine, he will have me.

He will have me.

This I swear.

Nurse Thompson had come out after a while—presumably, thought Rhianna, when she'd realised Alexis Petrakis was now with Nicky and Karen—and helped her back to her room. Had she heard that hideous scene out there? Rhianna wondered dully. It would be amazing if she had not—if the whole household had not.

But all Nurse Thompson said was, 'Bed. And you are not to move. You'll end up back in hospital if you carry on like this.'

Rhianna was docile, beyond protest. Beyond anything. But her brain was going round and round and round, like a rat in a trap.

But how? Where?

She felt so weak, so helpless, so ill.

And so completely, absolutely alone.

There was no one. No one.

Tiredness dragged at her, reminding her how weak she still was.

She went on lying in her bed, staring at the ceiling.

While she was weak like this she was helpless. She had to get well again, strong again. When she was strong—then she could fight Alexis Petrakis.

Fight him and win.

For Nicky's sake.

Alexis was working in his study after dinner, catching up with the essentials of Petrakis International via e-mail, fax and phone. He had spent the afternoon with Nicky, once he'd surfaced from his after-lunch nap. They'd gone swimming again, built a sandcastle and played football. Then he'd sat in on Nicky's supper, and read to him before bathtime.

A knock on the door interrupted him.

'Mr Petrakis?'

It was the nurse, standing in the doorway. She had a determined look on her face.

Alexis sat back, control in his movement.

'Yes?'

She advanced into the room with her stolid tread, closing the study door behind her.

'I must speak to you,' she announced.

He nodded. 'Very well.' His face was impassive.

She took a breath. There was a determined look on her face.

'My responsibility, as you will appreciate, is to my patient,' she began. 'And for that reason I must request that she is not subjected to...' The woman hesitated a moment, then continued, 'To the kind of emotional...upheavals...that have happened these last two days. Such episodes are not helpful to her recovery. She had been making excellent progress, but she is in significant danger of relapsing. I have had to sedate her again, and that is *not* conducive to her convalescence.'

Alexis's face was a mask. Choosing his words carefully, he answered.

'I appreciate your concern, Nurse Thompson. However, the best way to ensure the...tranquillity...of your patient is to keep her away from me.' Alexis felt the grip on his pen tighten as he spoke. Abruptly, he took the helm of this exchange. 'While you are here, Nurse, I want to understand precisely what your patient's medical condition is and how her treatment is being handled.' His voice was expressionless. 'You will understand, naturally, that an essential aspect of her treatment is to expedite her removal from drug dependency.'

The nurse raised her eyebrows. 'The dosages are declining, certainly, but she can't be taken off them too quickly or she could well relapse. Her body is still reliant on them.'

Alexis's face darkened. So much for Rhianna Davies's self-righteous denial that she was a drug-user.

'She's that severely addicted?' he demanded grimly.

The nurse's eyebrows rose even higher.

'Addicted? I don't understand.'

There was something in the woman's tone of voice that infuriated Alexis.

'If you'd taken the trouble to read her medical records you might know what I'm talking about!' he snapped at her icily.

The nurse bridled. 'There is absolutely nothing in her medical records to indicate she is a drug addict!'

'She was under the influence of drugs when she walked out in front of a car!'

Nurse Thompson took a deep breath. 'Mr Petrakis, a detailed medical examination was made when Ms Davies was admitted to the Accident and Emergency department of Sarmouth General Hospital. The only substance in her blood was an over-the-counter flu remedy! Far too much of it, but nothing, absolutely *nothing,* illicit. Nor did any of her very many subsequent medical examinations during her hospitalisation reveal the slightest sign that she is or was a substance-abuser. And *if* you do not believe me consult with your own Dr Paniotis,' she finished witheringly.

'She must have been high on something to walk out blindly in front of that car!'

Nurse Thompson looked at him disbelievingly.

'She was knocked down by a speeding car. There were witnesses to the accident and the driver was later arrested on a drink-driving charge. It is all documented, and I'm sure the Sarmouth police will confirm it to you if you insist!'

Alexis stared at the woman.

'Are you telling me,' he said slowly, 'that she is not a drug addict?'

'I most certainly am! I've never heard such nonsense in my life!'

'Her social worker—'

A harrumphing sound came from Nurse Thompson's throat.

'Her social worker,' Alexis continued tersely, 'said she had evidence of drug usage and violence.'

Another dismissive snort came from the nurse. She eyed Alexis beadily. 'I can assure you, Mr Petrakis, from all my considerable number of years in nursing, that my patient is neither violent nor a drug addict!'

Alexis ignored her indignation.

'Then why does she look like a walking corpse?' he demanded.

Nurse Thompson's chest swelled.

'Probably because she very nearly became one,' she riposted defensively. 'When she was admitted to hospital after being knocked down by that hit-and-run driver she was discovered to be suffering from a severe, long-standing and untreated lung infection, exacerbated by chronic exhaustion. It required urgent and continued medication—medication that is still continuing, though in ever-decreasing dosages, as I indicated. Given the state she was in when she was run down, I wonder she was still on her feet at all—and, far from being able to threaten anyone with a knife, I would be surprised to hear that she had the strength even to lift such a weapon, let alone use it!'

For a long moment Alexis said nothing. Nurse Thompson went on standing in front of him, breathing heavily. His eyes went to her. She didn't look like a fool.

But if she was telling the truth...?

He turned away, staring out of the window over the darkening sea.

Thoughts he did not want to think were circling slowly in his head. He needed to think them through alone.

'Thank you, Nurse Thompson. That will be all.'

His voice was remote as he dismissed her.

Rhianna had been telling the truth. It was a disturbing realisation.

'Mummy!'

'Hello, muffin. Did you have a good nap?'

Nicky climbed up into his mother's lap and snuggled for a moment. Rhianna smoothed his hair, ignoring the pressure of his body on her still tender ribs. She had spent the morning, just like the previous afternoon and evening, in bed—at Nurse Thompson's insistence. But after lunch she had been allowed to get up, and was now installed on the terrace.

'Yes, but I want to play now. On the beach. You come too.'

'Oh, darling, perhaps tomorrow.'

A mutinous look crossed Nicky's face.

'No—now!'

'Nicky, your mother needs to rest. You know that. Resting will make her better sooner.'

The deep, accented voice was firm, but not admonishing. Rhianna's eyes flew to where Alexis Petrakis stood in the doorway, watching them.

There was a strange expression in his face. Different from any she'd seen before.

He looked—guarded.

Assessing.

Instinctively her arms tightened around Nicky, as if protecting him from Alexis Petrakis. She hadn't laid eyes on him since that hideous exchange yesterday morning. Now her pulse-rate had risen automatically, and she could feel herself tense.

'She's always resting. Like Grandpa. He was always tired and resting. And then he…he…'

Nicky's little mouth quivered.

Rhianna's heart wrenched. She folded her arms more tightly around Nicky.

'Oh, sweetheart, I'm not ill like Grandpa was ill. I'm getting better all the time—I promise. Look, I'll come down after all—all right? You get down first.'

'One moment.'

Before she realised what he was doing Alexis had leant forward and lifted Nicky off her lap. Though she let go of Nicky as quickly as she could it wasn't in time to stop Alexis's bare arm brushing against her hand.

Every muscle in her body froze.

He set Nicky down.

'Go and tell Karen we're going down on the beach.'

He ruffled his son's hair. He did not know where the gesture had come from, it just had.

'With Mummy?'

Alexis nodded. Nicky ran off, cheerful again.

Alexis turned back to Rhianna.

'What's this about Nicky's grandfather being ill and, I assume, not getting better?'

The question came out of nowhere.

'No, he didn't.' Her voice was tight. She didn't want to think about her father, his difficult, long-drawn-out dying. And she certainly didn't want to talk about it to Alexis Petrakis.

'Nicky remembers him?'

'Yes.' Her voice was terse.

'When did he die?'

She didn't answer. Her throat was tight. Far too tight. Like a thick elastic band constricting her.

'Last month.'

'*What?*'

There was shock in Alexis's voice. She could hear it. But she couldn't do anything about it. He'd asked and she'd told him. God knows why he'd asked.

'You lost your father a handful of weeks ago?'

There was still shock, and incredulity, and something more in his demand.

Rhianna swallowed. The lump in her throat was worse.

'He was very ill. It was expected.'

'How long had he been ill?'

What the hell was this? she thought. The Spanish Inquisition?

'Years.'

'Years? What was he suffering from?'

A broken heart. It was true. Losing Davies Yacht Design had broken her father's heart. Living people were nothing compared to his yachts.

'He'd had heart problems for years. Heart attacks, strokes. That sort of stuff.'

She could feel Alexis's eyes boring down at her. She

wanted him to drop dead. Go away. Disappear. But he wouldn't. He just kept on at her.

'Increasingly common,' he observed, as though to say something—anything. He seemed to pause a moment. 'I did not know of your loss. Or that it was so recent.' There was a certain stiffness in the way he spoke.

'It was more of a release than anything. The end was...difficult.' She stared down at her lap.

'It always is.'

There was a terseness in the way he spoke that made her glance up suddenly. She saw a bleakness about him that made her start.

Then Nicky was trotting back out on the terrace.

'Come on, Mummy!'

He rushed off down to the beach.

Before she realised what was happening Rhianna felt an arm scoop around her back and under her knees. She was lifted up effortlessly, as if she were swansdown.

Shock transfixed her. Then, frantically, she started to try and free herself.

'Put me down! Please!'

Alexis stared down at her, motionless suddenly. There was hysteria in her voice.

'Let me go.'

Slowly, he lowered her to the ground.

'What—?'

She shrank away from him, backing up against the balustrade.

'Don't *touch* me!' she whispered.

She made her own way down on to the beach, across the sand, resolutely refusing to take the arm Alexis silently proffered. It was slow progress, but she did it, and she sank gratefully down on to the sand, where Nicky had started to dig.

Alexis hunkered down beside the small figure and set to. Like Nicky, he was in shorts and T-shirt.

Rhianna watched them. Gradually her raised heart-rate was slowing, her breathing easing. The sand was warm and soft under her bare shins. She slid out of her sandals and let the fine sand drift between her toes. The warm sun beat down from the blue sky—not hot, but with gentle heat.

Alexis Petrakis was digging as industriously as her son. Two sable heads were bent to their task, delving deep into the damp sand at the bottom of a large hole, chucking the sand aside.

As she watched something strange seemed to be happening to her. The two sable heads were so alike. So was the air of concentration. Her gaze slipped to Alexis Petrakis.

Nicky's father.

But I don't want him to be. I don't *want* him to be Nicky's father! she thought desperately.

But she could want all she liked and it would not make it less true. Alexis Petrakis was Nicky's father. His genes were in Nicky—their shared colouring was testimony to that. And as she studied their industrious faces she felt her breath catch. It was more than the dark hair that made them look similar. There was something in the eyes, the shape of the mouth, the contours of the cheeks, that echoed each other. Words drifted back to her—Alexis Petrakis telling her that he had recognised Nicky instantly from his resemblance to himself when young.

Her mouth thinned. Alexis Petrakis could never have been young. He could never have been as Nicky was now, a loving, affectionate, vulnerable child…

Yet he looked different now from the way he usually looked.

He looked younger, she thought suddenly, even though he was nearly five years older than when she'd first seen him. Maybe it was just because he was wearing casual beach clothes, not the sophisticated tuxedo he'd been wearing when—

No. Don't think about that. Don't remember it.

But memories stole back. Not the hideous, ghastly morning after, but to the evening before.

He'd just been so incredibly attractive, she hadn't been able to drag her eyes from him for a moment. And she still couldn't.

Her eyes flickered over his face. He was in three-quarter profile and she could see the cut of his cheekbones, the strong slash of his nose, the arc of his brows, the set of his mouth. She wanted to go on staring. Just staring.

Something stirred deep within her. Something that had been dormant for a long, long time. For five long, bitter, grinding years.

She didn't want to feel it. Didn't want it stirring. Waking.

But it did all the same. Like a flickering heat somewhere deep, deep within her.

She dragged her eyes away from him, back to Nicky.

His son.

Our son.

Oh, God, Nicky was their son—they had created him between them. Created him on that night that had melted her like wax in his arms.

The night had been magical, wonderful, incandescent. She had never known, never dreamt it was possible to feel the way she had.

And yet for him it had never been intended as anything more than a one-night stand—a casual appetite for a woman easily sated.

But if it hadn't…?

What if that night, five long years ago, had been something quite, quite different?

Her eyes saw them both. Alexis and Nicky.

Her heart clenched, stopping the blood. A mirage floated in her vision. Alexis, her husband, and Nicky, the son they had created together on the first, wonderful night of many, many nights together. They could have been a family together, warm and loving and happy…

The mirage faded. Her heart started to beat again in dull, heavy slugs.

Alexis Petrakis had used her, then thrown her from him the next morning with the harshest, most unjust condemnation. Refusing to let her explain, justify herself.

He wasn't fit to be her son's father.

And yet...

She watched them digging, working as a team together, discussing the depth and size of the hole. Quite easy in each other's company.

The admission came unwillingly, but it came.

She might loathe Alexis Petrakis, might wish with all her heart that he was not the father of her son, but for all that she could not deny—quite extraordinarily—he was good with Nicky. Nicky was responding to him, she could see. It was nothing overt, nothing emotional. But Nicky had...accepted him.

She felt her heart twist suddenly. Nicky didn't even know who this man was. Still didn't know that the man digging a hole in the sand with him was his father.

A new thought came to her.

Maybe Alexis Petrakis wasn't planning on telling him after all. Maybe he was still thinking about whether to acknowledge him as his son.

Supposing he does and then changes his mind?

Her stomach clenched. Far, far worse than not knowing who your father was would be knowing your father had rejected you.

As if you weren't good enough for him.

As if you'd failed him.

Emotion knifed through her. Emotion and memory.

Nicky scrambled to his feet.

'I want to put water in!' he announced. He seized his bucket and raced to the sea's edge.

Before she could stop herself Rhianna heard herself blurting out, as Nicky ran out of earshot.

'You're not going to acknowledge him, are you? He's not going to know you're his father, is he?'

Alexis's head swivelled to her.

'Nicky will know I am his father. When I judge the time to be right I will tell him,' he said grimly.

'You can't change your mind once he knows. You know that, don't you? You can't decide later that you don't want to be his father any more.'

There was sharpness in her voice. And fear too.

He looked at her, eyes narrowed.

Assessing.

The way he'd looked at her when he'd come out on the terrace.

'I have no intention of doing so. Nicky is my son for ever.' His voice became grim suddenly. 'Every boy needs a father. Something you callously chose to ignore. His needs are paramount. Which is why you will stay with Nicky while he needs you—'

'He'll *always* need me. I'm his *mother!*'

His jaw tightened. 'While he needs you, he has you.' His eyes flashed again, dark fire. 'I would *never* part a child from its mother—even if she wanted to leave him!'

Rhianna stared at him incredulously.

'*No* woman leaves her child!'

There was a sudden night-black tension in his face.

'Some do. Some women have no maternal instinct. It is a quality absent from their beings.'

Rhianna bit her lip. 'Then they don't have children.'

'Don't they?' The dark of his eyes seemed to be burning with a blackness that was impenetrable. That reached down into the depths.

Something shuddered deep inside her. Then, like the breaking of a tautening wire, Nicky was stumbling towards them with his bucket slopping water, and Alexis turned his attention away from her.

Back to his son.

Nicky was pouring the water into the hole. He watched it a moment, then announced.

'It's going away!'

'It won't stay, Nicky,' Alexis told him. 'It's draining into the sand.'

'But I want it to stay!' Nicky exclaimed indignantly.

'We can't always have what he want,' he replied.

His eyes flickered towards the woman who sat, legs curled under her, on the sand. No, you couldn't always have what you wanted.

He didn't want Rhianna Davies to be Nicky's mother, but she was.

He watched her a moment. Her face was shuttered and tense, not looking anywhere near him. She was still thin, but she was no longer the death's head she'd been when he'd first laid eyes on her in hospital.

A frown darkened his eyes.

It hadn't been drugs that had made her look so ill.

When the nurse had so soundly refuted this, he'd contacted Dr Paniotis and he had confirmed this morning that there was no evidence of drug abuse by Rhianna Davies. What the social worker had found in her flat had simply been flu powder. And she had, indeed, been suffering from a serious untreated lung infection before she'd been knocked down on a pedestrian crossing by a drunk speeding driver.

Which meant that it had not been her fault she'd ended up in hospital looking like a death's head. Which meant—

His mind veered off the path it was leading him down. No, he would not feel compunction. Nor pity for her. He could be glad, yes, for Nicky's sake, that at least she wasn't a drug addict, but that in no way exonerated her from the rest of her crimes.

He glanced covertly at her again, seeing the lines around her mouth, her eyes.

Chronic exhaustion, her medical records stated, on top of being ill and injured.

He frowned again. Why had she made no mention of the fact that her father had died so recently? Or that he'd been ill for so long.

He knew how much of a strain it could be when a parent was ill for years. With his father, it had taken two years from his first heart attack to his final fatal one, and the time had stretched endlessly. His father had refused to acknowledge his 'weakness', as he'd called it, and insisted on keeping all the reins of power of Petrakis International. Yet his obsessive determination to stay at the helm had inevitably shortened his life. Nor had he let his son take some of the pressure from him.

His son? Alexis's mouth twisted suddenly. His father's final bitter words to him, as he had surfaced, so briefly, from his last massive attack, reverberated in his mind.

Instinctively, his eyes went back to Nicky.

My son, he thought. *My son.*

Emotion, fierce and protective, surged through him.

CHAPTER SIX

'GOODNIGHT, my darling.' Rhianna smoothed her sleeping son's hair one last time, a huge, unending wave of love and protection pouring from her. Nothing would take him from her again. Not principalities nor powers.

And not Alexis Petrakis.

He says he won't part you, though. He says while Nicky needs you he will have you...

And you trust him? You actually trust a man like that? Who did what he did to you? Pain stabbed at her, twisting like a knife.

How could he have been so callous to her? How could he have treated her like that?

The answer came cold and clear, the way it always did.

Hurting her more than anything else.

Because you were just a one-night stand. Casual sex. No one important...

She got to her feet. Well, now she was his son's mother.

And Alexis Petrakis was no one important to her.

Except as a man who threatened her and her son.

She straightened her shoulders and walked into her bedroom.

Nurse Thompson was in there.

'Nicky asleep? Good. Now, tonight, I understand, you are to eat in the dining room?'

Her voice was bland. Rhianna stared. She usually ate her evening meal with Nurse Thompson and Karen, in their sitting room, chatting amicably about anything that had nothing to do with why Rhianna was here on a privately owned Greek island with a child who looked like the man who owned it.

After eating they watched English-language satellite channels. It was relaxing, easy and familiar.

But maybe, she thought viciously as she headed haltingly for the dining room across the central hallway, Alexis Petrakis didn't like the idea of her getting cosy with those whom he had hired—as he had so scathingly informed her—to supervise her contact with her son. Maybe now she was supposed to eat in isolation, on her own.

Or maybe not.

He was waiting for her, standing by the sideboard and pouring himself a whisky.

Abruptly she turned to go.

'What are you doing?' The voice was sharp.

'Going to my room.'

An exasperated sigh escaped Alexis's lips.

'Stavros is about to serve dinner.'

'I don't want any.'

His voice darkened. 'We have things to talk about.'

Rhianna whirled round as fast as her legs would bear.

'No, we don't. The only talking I'll do with you now, after what you've said to me, is through a lawyer. Nicky is my son. I have custody of him. And you—as you have already admitted—have no rights in law over him. So don't even think of using your wealth and power to take him from me!'

Her voice had risen. Adrenaline surged within her. It was the flight-or-fight hormone, but there was only one way she was going to use it. Her son was at stake—she had to fight for him. Had to.

'Understand this, and understand it well: Nicky is my *life*. I will keep him safe till my dying day. I will not let you take him from me—part him from me—in any way separate him from me. I will not let you be the cause of a single tear, a single moment of grief or loss, a single moment of fear for him. Because if you are, I will see you burn in hell, Alexis Petrakis! As God is my witness, you will burn in hell!'

Ferocity contorted her face, her breathing heavy and laboured with the effort of her vehemence.

But Alexis was just staring at her. As if someone completely new had just stepped out to berate him.

A mother—fighting for her child—tooth and nail and claw—with all her might.

It could just be an act.

The cold, cynical voice spoke inside him. She heard what you said about some women not being maternal, so she's standing there doing a number to show how devoted she is.

His eyes rested on her, assessing, judgmental. The outburst had seemed ao genuine, so passionate. So absolute. What was it about this woman that confused his judgement, his instincts, so powerfully?

But was it the truth?

Was Rhianna Davies a devoted mother? Or had she been hiding Nicky? Biding her time before cashing in on him?

But why—why wait so long, living in poverty, before producing his son?

The words she had hurled at him—that she would never have told him he was Nicky's father—circled in his brain. Why had she said that?

And why was she living in such poverty? He'd assumed it was because of her drug addiction—yet she wasn't an addict, never had been. So why live in a council flat on benefits? Her father had owned a company; she'd been wearing a designer dress the evening she'd targeted him for her scheme.

None of it made sense.

He wanted answers.

That was why he was prepared to have dinner with her like this.

She was opening the door, about to walk out on him. Rapidly he strode across the room, shutting the door with the flat of his hand. He laid a restraining hand on her arm. She flung him off jerkily.

'Don't touch me!' she spat.

His mouth tightened, but he let her go. She looked as if she was about to fall over; if she wanted to do so on her own she was welcome.

'Sit down before you fall down. I have questions to ask you and I want answers.'

Balefully, she sank down on a chair. Yelling at him like that had exhausted her.

He took his place opposite her, moodily taking a mouthful of whisky, then looking grimly at her.

Now what? she thought bitterly. What vile accusation can he throw at me this time?

But when he spoke it was the very last thing she had expected.

He set down his whisky glass with a click.

'It would seem,' he said, and his voice was very dry, 'that I have been misinformed about you. Your medical records show you are not, after all, a drug addict.'

Rhianna stared across at him.

'That was very thorough of you,' she said. Sarcasm was heavy in her voice, but relief flickered through.

Alexis frowned. 'Nor,' he went on, 'does it seem you behaved recklessly with my son's life the day of your accident. Moreover, you had apparently been suffering a severe and dangerous chest infection for some time, to which doubtless the strain of your father's death—something else I was not informed of—contributed.'

He made it sound as if the lack of information was her fault, Rhianna thought balefully.

He reached forward to take another mouthful of whisky. Then, with a click, he set back the glass.

'Tell me, why are you living in a council flat on state benefit?'

Her eyes flashed.

'Is that a serious question?' she retorted derisively.

A flicker of annoyance showed in his face.

'Just answer me.'

'Because I have no other means of support.'

She didn't owe him the truth, she didn't owe him a cent, but he could have the truth and choke on it for all she cared.

'Why not? Are you estranged from your family?'

'There was only my father. He had no means of support either.'

Alexis sat back.

'He owned a yacht design company. I remember that quite clearly. It was, after all, the reason you came on to me. So there must have been money around.' It was his turn for sarcasm to be heavy in his voice.

She had gone white. Every bone in her face was standing out as if she were a skeleton.

'You *bastard!*'

It was a hiss as venomous as a snake's.

'What?' His brows had snapped together.

'My father lost his company and every other possession! He had *nothing*. We lived on my single parent income support in my single parent council accommodation—'

'Is this the truth?'

Rhianna erupted.

'What the hell do you mean, is that the truth? Of course it's the truth! He went bankrupt when MML pulled the plug on the takeover—at your orders! He had nothing left. Everything was secured against the company's borrowings, and it all went! Even his house. He had to come and live with me. He had nowhere else to go!'

'Your father lived with you?'

'No, he lived in Buckingham Palace!'

He ignored her bitter rejoinder. 'I didn't know.'

She stopped. Emotions were flowing with memory, and both were agonising.

To her relief, the door to the kitchen quarters opened and Stavros entered, bearing a tray with soup tureens and a basket of bread. By the time he'd finished serving them Rhianna's composure had painfully returned.

She started to eat. She was hungry, she realised. The delicate lemon-scented chicken soup was delicious, and slipped down her tight, taut throat. So did the fish, grilled with herbs and served with fragrant rice.

They did not talk. Rhianna could only be grateful. Across from her, Alexis had a closed, shuttered look on his face.

She went on eating.

The last time you shared a meal in Alexis's company he took you to bed afterwards...

Of their own volition her eyes stole to him. She felt a slow, powerful tremor go through her.

He was having just the same effect on her now as he had had five years ago.

She tried to stop herself looking, but she couldn't. The sable hair, the strong planes of his face, the straight nose, the sculpted mouth and, oh, those dark gold-flecked eyes with their long, long lashes...

How could she have hoped to resist him? For five long years she had coruscated herself for her shaming, shameful weakness that night. To have fallen like a ripe peach into his arms, his bed, revelling in what he did to her, burning like a flame in his embrace.

But now, sitting here, seeing him again, she knew exactly how it was she had been so very, very easy for him to seduce.

Yet she still could never, never forgive herself for what she had done. What she had let him do.

All for the sake of a cheap, meaningless one-night stand.

Guilt and shame burned through her.

Well, she thought with bitter satisfaction, she was safe from him now. She didn't need a mirror to tell her what he saw when he looked at her.

She could see it in his eyes.

Revulsion.

* * *

Alexis consumed his fish in silence. His mind was preoccupied.

So Davies Yacht Design had been on the point of total collapse when Rhianna Davies had used him. She hadn't given the impression they were that desperate for investment. But then his business brain clicked in. For her to have done so would have been to weaken her hand. No company wanting a life-saving bail-out would want a potential investor to realise just how critical the situation was.

But if MML had been keen to buy Davies Yacht Design it must have had potential, as she'd claimed, for returning on the investment. Had it not been for his standard policy of freezing the investment plans of any company newly acquired by Petrakis International, MML would probably have gone through with the takeover.

'After the buy-out fell through why didn't your father line up another white knight—or was the mess worse than you've admitted?'

Rhianna's head jerked up.

'Because he had another heart attack the day after I—after you—' She stopped, the words cutting off.

'Another?' Alexis's voice was strangely expressionless. He set down his knife and fork.

Rhianna swallowed. Why was he putting her through this?

'He'd had a heart attack three days before—' Again she stopped.

'Your father had just had a heart attack when you approached me at that dinner?'

She gritted her teeth. 'Yes. He was in Intensive Care. I had no choice but to try and talk to you like that at the dinner. The banks were going to foreclose the following week unless the takeover got the go-ahead at MML. Your PA let slip that you would be going to that dinner that night—I'd asked if I could have an evening appointment to see you, but she said your schedule was already finalised. So—' she took a harsh breath '—I bought a ticket for the dinner, and altered the seating plan on the board at the cocktail reception beforehand so I could make sure I was on your table. It was my last chance. I had nothing to lose.'

She fell silent.

She had been wrong. She had had a lot to lose—and she had lost it all.

Slowly Alexis digested what she had just said.

Her father in Intensive Care with a heart attack. The banks about to foreclose.

She must have been desperate...

Was that why she had done what she had? Offered him the one thing she had left? The traditional last coinage of every woman. Her body.

Then his eyes hardened. However desperate she'd been she should not have tried to take him for a gullible fool she could manipulate with her sexual favours!

'And the idea of simply asking me to consider the takeover on its own merit never occurred to you, did it?'

'I beg your pardon?' Rhianna's voice was hollow.

'Had you not assumed that you could use your body to persuade me to look favourably on the takeover—'

Rage exploded through her.

'How dare you make such an accusation? I *never* at any time thought such a thing, intended such a thing, or *did* such a thing! My God, you are a vile, disgusting man!'

A palm slammed down on the table-top.

'I was *there!* I witnessed every feminine trick and wile you played on me!'

'I didn't do anything!' she protested.

He laughed, coarsely and derisively, leaning back in his chair, his meal totally abandoned now.

'You left not one trick unplayed!' His voice was excoriating. 'The wide eyes, the breathy voice, the low-cut gown, the long blonde hair, the skin-tight dress. All that eye contact and come-hither gazing you did over dinner. You asked to speak to me *privately* and came up to my suite without blinking! What the hell did you think you were going to do there? Present your business case? Quote me net present values and projected earnings? No, the only thing you were going to present me with was your body! Which you did—very lavishly—having first ensured you'd whetted my appetite for it to the maximum by spilling champagne over your breasts so that I could see them in their full glory. Then you came on to me like a—'

Her fist closed around her wine glass. She hurled the contents at him.

'You *lying* bastard! It was *you!* You came on to me! *You*—'

She never finished. He was on his feet, towering over her across the table. The wine had splashed across his shirt-front, plastering it to his chest. His expression was savage. So was his voice and his words.

'Don't try and rewrite the truth!' he snarled at her. 'We both know what the truth is. You used me. Calculatingly. Deliberately. For your own ends.'

She pushed her chair back, struggling to her feet. Her face was convulsed with fury. Five long years of fury.

The crack of her hand across his cheek was like a pistol-shot. His head jerked back. His eyes were like twin satanic fires. Burning with hellfire.

'You *disgust* me!' she hissed. 'You dare to try and put the blame on me? The only, *only* reason I came to your suite was to try and get you to listen to my business case. *There was no other reason!* How dare you accuse me of anything else?'

His eyes flickered with that dark satanic light.

'How dare I? Tell me, if you are so right and I am so wrong, how come you tumbled right down into my bed the way you did?'

Her eyes spat at him.

'Because I was *stupid*. Stupid and naive and…and…' Her head sank. 'Because I was stupid,' she said again, her voice suddenly dull, and dead. She lifted her head again. It seemed as heavy as lead. Her whole body seemed as heavy as lead. What the hell was she doing, trying to justify herself to this man? She owed him nothing. Nothing at all. Her eyes rested on him. They were full of contempt and loathing.

'It doesn't matter whether you believe me or not. I only care about Nicky. He's all I care about in the whole world.'

She stumbled away from the table, her legs jerky, her breathing like knives in her chest. She didn't care. She had to get away—away. That was all.

He watched her go. Adrenaline surging in his body. He wanted to follow her and shake her until he had shaken the truth out of her—until she'd admitted what she'd done. But she was hardly able to make it to the door. Like a broken puppet with the strings cut.

When she had gone, leaving the door open, and he could hear her stumbling across the corridor that led to the bedrooms, he sat down heavily again. With a dark, vicious look on his face he reached for the wine bottle.

CHAPTER SEVEN

MOONLIGHT glimmered on the water. A chilly little wind played about his face. Wavelets lapped in the dark by his feet.

Alexis stared out over the sea, hands gripping the edge of the balustrade on the terrace. The boats of fishermen were dotted about, their lights luring the fish.

He was calm now. Back under control.

But he had come very close to losing control completely.

It had been her defiance—her refusal to admit the truth about that night five long years ago. Insisting on her innocence—insisting she had never set out to exploit her sexual allure the way he *knew* she had. Oh, she had been skilful, all right—had he not had his illusions ripped from him in the morning he would have gone on being fooled by her.

Cold ran through him. He had come within a hair's breadth of making an irreversible fool of himself over her. That morning, when he'd woken her with a kiss, her warm, soft sensuality had nearly persuaded him to abandon the business meeting in his diary and stay with her until his flight left at lunchtime.

He gave a harsh, self-mocking laugh.

Thee mou, he'd been going to take her back to Greece with him! One night with her had been no way enough! He'd wanted far, far more than that.

How much more?

He stared out to sea.

That night had been something extraordinary, unique. She had been like no woman he had ever known. Ardent, enraptured, giving herself to him so totally, so absolutely, that it had taken his breath away.

He had stood, he knew, on the shore of a sea, ready to plunge into its unknown depths and discover—

Discover something that had never existed for him before.

His palms clenched over the cold stone.

Instead he had discovered, in the morning, that he was simply a fool.

Manipulated by a woman for her own ends.

Just as his father had been.

Memory flickered in his mind. He put it from him, but it intruded again.

He saw it fresh in his mind's eye. Heard it. Heard that crack like a pistol-shot, as clearly now as if the intervening decades had never been, as the palm of his father's hand slashed across his mother's face.

Heard the word that went with the pistol-shot. At five he hadn't known what it was, but now he knew.

'Bitch!'

All he'd known then was the fear. The terror. And the rage—the rage that had made him rush to his father, battering at his legs.

'Don't hit my mummy! Don't hit her!'

His father had put him aside. His mother hadn't even looked at him. Instead she'd simply lifted her chin, ignoring her reddening cheek, and opened her leather handbag with a click of her manicured scarlet nails. She'd dropped the piece of paper his father had given her inside. Then she'd given a little smile. Not to him. To his father.

'Goodbye, Georgiou,' she'd said. 'Enjoy the boy. After all, you've paid enough for him. Even though he isn't yours.'

She'd walked away, shutting the door behind her with a click.

He'd watched her go. He hadn't understood.

He'd turned to his father.

'When is Mummy coming back?'

His father hadn't answered. Alexis had looked up at his

face and it had been like stone. Suddenly his father had looked down at him.

The expression in his face had terrified him.

It had been filled with hate.

'Never.'

His voice had been hard. Like iron. Then he'd walked away as well. Into another room. Another click of the door.

His five-year-old self had stood still for quite some time.

After a while, a servant had come and led him away.

But his father had spoken the truth. He had never seen his mother again.

It was strange, he thought now, three decades later, how pain could live like memory—quite blotted out, yet instantly there once more, like memory recalled.

His hands clenched, every muscle in his body seizing as if in spasm. He kept staring out to sea.

The pain was his—but it would never, ever be his son's.

Again that fierce protective surge went through him. He would protect his son from all that could hurt him.

Like an echo, he heard in his head the vehement vow his son's mother had given—*Nicky is my life. I will keep him safe till my dying day. I will not let you be the cause of a single tear, a single moment of grief or loss, a single moment of fear for him!*

She'd sounded so vehement, so convincing. But had it all been calculated, fake?

Can I trust her? Trust her to love Nicky the way she claims she does?

That was the question that went round and round in his head.

He went on staring out to sea, the cold lapping at him.

And as he stared he knew, finally, that he *had* to know.

Had to know whether Rhianna Davies loved his son.

There was only one way to find out. Only one way to know the truth.

*   *   *

Rhianna was having breakfast with Nicky out on the sunny terrace. She felt tired and drained after the ugliness of the scene the night before. Yet another scene. Yet another vicious exchange of venom and hatred.

Yet Nicky, blessedly, was unscarred.

She watched him diligently throwing breadcrumbs to the tiny sparrows that darted from the balustrade to the paved floor to pick them up. He was chattering happily about watching the helicopter land that morning with Karen. Rhianna listened with half an ear, nodding and responding as necessary. But there was a heaviness in her heart.

He mustn't be hurt. Whatever happens—however foul Alexis Petrakis is to me, however hard I have to fight back against him—Nicky mustn't be hurt.

There were footsteps approaching, and she looked away from Nicky.

Alexis came out on the terrace.

Nicky's face lit up.

'Can we play?' he asked immediately, starting to slide off his chair. 'I've finished my breakfast, Mummy.'

Alexis came up to him. He ignored Rhianna.

He smiled down at his son.

'What would you like to play first?'

'Swimming! Football! Sandcastles!' responded Nicky at once, then added as a dutiful afterthought, 'Please.'

Rhianna saw Alexis laugh, his face lightening.

She felt something clench inside.

It was that different person again, she thought. The one Nicky saw—but never her.

Would you want to? Why should you? Alexis Petrakis is nothing to you—nothing except your enemy. Don't crave smiles from him.

Not that she would get them. Alexis Petrakis directed only one thing at her.

Condemnation.

He was speaking again—to his son.

'We can do them all—but first you need to put your swimming trunks on and get Karen to put your sunblock on.'

Nicky was off like a shot.

'Don't forget to brush your teeth,' Rhianna called out after him.

'Bleah!' cried Nicky, as he ran indoors to find his nanny.

Rhianna brought her gaze back, to find that Alexis was looking down at her.

Her expression stilled, became impassive. He was going to say something vile, she could tell. But then, when did he ever say anything to her that was not vile?

'If you have finished your breakfast too, I should like to speak to you.'

She eyed him stonily, saying nothing.

'In my office,' said Alexis.

Now what? she thought bitterly. What else is he going to throw at me? Threaten me with?

She steeled herself. Her only option was to fight—every inch of the way.

She got to her feet carefully. The pain in her lungs was easing day by day, but her muscles had tensed at the coming ordeal.

He led the way back inside, across the hall to a room she had never been into. As she followed, at her slower, halting pace, she realised why. It was his space. A sleek PC dominated a large desk. Alexis Petrakis was already behind it. A maroon leather folder lay on the surface of the desk in front of him.

A bad feeling started to pool inside her.

'Sit down.'

His manner was different this morning, she thought. She didn't know why, but it was. And there was something about it that made her feel very, very uneasy.

Impassively she lowered herself to the chair in front of the desk.

Was this deliberate intimidation? she wondered. Making

her sit meekly while he lorded it behind his desk? Well, she would not be intimidated. Must not be.

'I have a proposition to put to you.'

His voice was inexpressive. So was his face. His eyes were shuttered.

He flicked open the folder. There was a document inside, and a piece of smaller paper on the top.

It was a cheque, Rhianna could see.

'I am prepared,' said Alexis Petrakis, in a voice devoid of emotion, 'to hand over to you the sum of twenty million pounds. In exchange you will sign all custody rights to my son to me—in perpetuity. Doing so will make you a very rich woman.' He paused. 'As part of this exchange you will be available to Nicky, on demand, for as long as he wants you. However, there will be certain restrictions on your freedom of action. You will not be permitted to contact the press, you will not be permitted to lead a life that will cause embarrassment or distress to my son, and all your contact with him will be under supervision—either by myself or my nominee.

'The sum of twenty million pounds will be held for you, in a high-yield investment portfolio, the interest from which will be yours to spend as you will, and the capital sum, compounded over the years, will become yours outright on Nicky's majority. By this arrangement you will gain a highly luxurious lifestyle, with the expectation of a very generous fortune in fourteen years' time, yet Nicky will be assured of the continued presence of his mother in his life, while he wants that.'

He paused again, then went on, his voice still completely businesslike, as though he were unveiling normal terms and conditions. 'This document, which I have had flown here this morning, details the financial disposition I have just outlined. Feel free to peruse it carefully.' His voice drained of expression even more. 'In addition, I am prepared to issue this cheque, cashable immediately, as a gesture of good faith on my part, for your co-operation in this agreement. It is in the sum of two million pounds and is yours outright. Right now.'

The obsidian eyes rested on her. Nothing showed in them whatsoever.

For one beat of a heart, Rhianna paused. Then, in a composed voice, she spoke.

'May I see?'

Silently, he pushed the folder across to her. His face was like carved stone. Still nothing showed in his eyes. Nothing at all. And yet something was there. She could see. Something.

But she did not know what.

Nor did she care.

She lifted the cheque, drawn on his personal account at a historic London private bank. She glanced at it, then set it aside. Then she picked up the document underneath, leafing through it.

Then she replaced it on the table. Put the cheque on top of it. She picked them both up again and, with jagged, violent movements, tore them into fragments, scattering them on the gleaming polished surface of the desk.

She got to her feet.

Slowly, succinctly, banking down every single sign of any emotion in her whatsoever, she spoke.

'I will say this to you very clearly. So that even someone as vile as you can understand. My son is not for sale. Not—for—sale. And if you *ever* make such an attempt again, I will—'

She broke off. Emotion erupted within her. Unstoppable. Overpowering. Hatred poured from her like a dark, black tide.

Forcibly she took a sharp, scything breath that cut her lungs like glass.

'You are a monster,' she breathed. 'A sick, degenerate, disgusting monster. There are no depths that you would not stoop to. It makes me ill to breathe the same air as you.'

She fumbled her way to the door, reaching for the handle blindly. But as she did there seemed to be a great, crushing heaviness bowing her down. So great she could not bear it, could not breathe.

Oh, God—that such a man should have fathered Nicky. Prepared to buy his own son from her. Thinking he was for sale.

That she would sell her son to him.

How can I bear it? she thought, the heaviness crushing her. How can I bear Nicky being near such a man? Being his son?

There was something thick in her lungs, in her throat. Something that was choking her, filling up in her, trying to break out, spill over, escape.

But she mustn't let it escape. Not here, not now, not in front of such a man. Such a monster. Who had fathered her son and now wanted to buy him.

Her hand closed around the handle, but she could not turn it. Could not move. Could only feel that choking, cracking feeling in her lungs, her throat.

She leant against the door panel, weakness convulsing through her, making her shake and tremble.

The first sob tore from her even as Alexis thrust back his chair, and hurried to her.

CHAPTER EIGHT

SHE wouldn't let him help her. Wouldn't let him guide her back to the chair. Wouldn't let him hold her.

She shrank away from him, clutching the door, in physical and emotional collapse.

'Don't touch me!' Her voice was a yell, a screech, convulsed with a high, racking sobbing.

She shook his hands from her forcibly, trying to yank the door open. But her eyes were blind, her hands shaking, her limbs trembling. Unable to get the door open, she spun round, reeling, backing against the closed door like an animal at bay.

Because that was what she was. A wretched, hunted antelope that the leopard in front of her wanted to devour, tear apart, destroy completely.

The sobs were choking in her throat as she held her hands up to ward him off.

'Keep away from me! Keep *away* from me!'

She couldn't take any more—she just could not. She was hitting out at him, not impacting, but sweeping her arms in front of her to keep him away.

He stood stock still. Emotion was knifing through him, and he could not tell what it was. He had no time to think about it. She was going out of control, he could see, and collapsing visibly in front of her eyes. He turned on his heel and snatched up the house phone on his desk, barking something in Greek down the line. Then he turned round again.

'Nurse Thompson is coming. She will look after you. If you stand aside from the door she can come in. I—I will not touch you.'

Her breathing, through the harsh, choking sobs, was gasping. He could see her chest rising and falling jerkily. A knock sounded sharply on the door from the outside.

'That is Nurse Thompson. If you just step to one side she can come in.'

She did what he told her, rolling her body so that she was half collapsed against the wall beside the door. Nurse Thompson pushed it open carefully and, to his relief, took over immediately. With brisk, controlled movements she guided the sobbing, choking figure outside, paying no attention to the man standing there, rigidly immobile, witnessing the scene.

When she had gone, he shut the door behind her. He walked back heavily to his chair behind the desk and sank down on it. On the surface of the desk the torn document and cheque curled, despised and rejected. He sat still, looking at the sorry remains. Then slowly, methodically, he gathered up the shards and swept them into a wastepaper basket.

They would not be needed again.

'Where's Nicky?'

Rhianna's voice was faint, but fearful, urgent. Nurse Thompson answered calmly. 'Karen is reading to him. He's quite content. Just rest now.'

Rest. It was the only thing she could do. It was as if a steamroller had just gone over her. But then that was what Alexis Petrakis was. A savage-toothed, crushing steamroller that would crush her and tear her if she let him.

Fear convulsed through her. More than fear. Revulsion.

Revulsion at a man who could stoop so low as to think a child was for sale...

Her mind writhed in powerless torment. She *had* to get away from here! She *had* to!

The door of the bedroom opened. Rhianna's eyes shot towards it, and Nurse Thompson's bulky figure also turned in that direction.

Alexis Petrakis stood there. He looked taller, darker, yet

there was something about him that was different. Rhianna didn't know what. Didn't care what.

'Nurse, I would like a few minutes alone with your patient, if you please.'

It might have been phrased as a request, but Nurse Thompson heard it as an order. For a moment she held her employer's eyes.

'Ms Davies is *not* to be further distressed,' she informed one of the richest men in Greece.

Gravely, Alexis Petrakis inclined his head.

'I shall not do so,' he replied. Then his gaze slipped past the nurse, on to the woman lying on the bed. Again, through the tension that had instantly stiffened her body as he had entered the room, Rhianna felt something different about him. But fear and tension overlaid everything, blotting out any recognition of what that difference was.

Briefly, Nurse Thompson nodded, and stalked out of the room. As the door shut behind her Alexis Petrakis stepped forward. Automatically, Rhianna sought to back against the pillows propping her up.

Now what was he going to do? Dear God, how much more of this could she stand?

He was standing at the foot of the bed, looking down at her. She felt a shiver go through her. For what seemed like a long, timeless moment he said nothing, just stood there, tall, dark, his face shuttered, unreadable. Then, abruptly, he spoke.

'It would appear,' he said, and there was a tightness in his voice that made it sound strange, forbidding, 'that I have been wrong about you.'

She said nothing, only felt her fingers clench into the coverlet laid over her.

Something moved in his eyes. Again she could not tell what. The tension lacing through her did not allow for any analysis.

'Not in everything,' he went on—and in those few words

she heard unmistakably that note of harsh condemnation she had become so familiar with in his accusing exchanges with her. 'But in one essential area.' He paused a moment, and Rhianna became aware that his fingers were clenched tightly at his sides.

His voice changed. Became strained, not harsh.

'You do, after all, seem to care for Nicky.'

Rhianna's eyes widened. She could not help it. Stupefied, she stared at the man standing at the end of the bed.

'I thought it a show—a parade of false emotionality—put on deliberately to up your value, present yourself in a good light to me. Bid up your price.'

His voice was drained of emotion, and Rhianna felt the breath stop in her lungs.

'But you turned down twenty-two million pounds for him. That—' suddenly his breath rasped sharply, slamming down his emotions '—is very convincing.' He paused, taking in another sharp breath. 'So convincing that I am now prepared to…re-evaluate…my estimation of you.' Again the harshness entered his voice. 'Although I can never forgive you for keeping my son from me, nor for the manner of his conception, I do now accept that you do, indeed, care for him more than the wealth his paternity promises you. Accordingly, I now wish to make a…' he paused, then continued. 'A rapprochement…with you. For Nicky's sake, he cannot have parents at war with one another. It is too distressing for him—too destructive.'

There was an edge in his voice like the blade of a knife over vulnerable flesh.

'We must make an accommodation with each other for his sake. Present a front to him that, whilst not idyllic, nevertheless will not blight his childhood.' Dark, expressionless eyes bored down on her. 'Only one person is important here—and that is Nicky. Whatever our feelings about each other, they *must not* poison him. I will not allow it.' He took a final, sharp intake of breath. 'So, on this basis, I am prepared to move forward.

'For now,' he continued, his voice changing minutely, 'your focus must be to recover your health. Mine will be to continue to get to know my son. This will also—' his mouth tightened '—give us the opportunity to…accommodate… each other.'

His eyes flickered over her assessingly, taking in her blank, hostile expression.

'I would appreciate it,' he said, the edge coming back to his voice, 'if there is a concomitant effort made on your part. All that is required is common civility—'

'Civility?' Her voice was thin. She was finally finding her words now, after the sheer stupefaction she had felt at hearing what he was saying to her. 'You expect civility from me— after what you've said to me, what you've done to me? Threatening me, verbally abusing me, haranguing me—'

His expression stiffened.

'I accept now that much of what I feared to be true about you is not so—'

'Well, everything I feared to be true about you *is* so!' she shot back, venom in her voice as she struggled to sit up properly. 'You are *every* bit as foul as I thought. Throwing your filthy accusations at me, time and again.'

Alexis's eyes flashed with instant anger. Then, visibly, he controlled it.

'I have just said that I accept that I was mistaken—'

'And *I've* just said that I wasn't! You tried to buy my son. What the *hell* kind of man does that?'

His expression tensed. His eyes became opaque. He couldn't tell her that he'd experienced it himself, had been put through that torment.

'I had to be sure. Sure that it wasn't just my money you were after. I had to make you choose between Nicky and money—'

Her eyes widened in horror.

'You deliberately offered me that stinking money to see if I would sell my son to you? It was just some kind of disgusting *test?*'

Emotion choked in her.

'I had to be sure, Rhianna—' His breath rasped again in his throat. 'And now that I am, we can, as I have come to make clear to you, move forward. Nicky needs us both. Both. And, however much neither of us wants to accept that, we must.' He shifted his weight on his feet. 'We must.

'I will leave you now, to think over what I have said. And please prepare yourself for one other thing. It is time I told Nicky that I am his father. I propose to do so this afternoon.' The dark eyes rested on her. 'It would be best if you were present. He may become confused, even distressed. But postponement will, I believe, only lead to greater confusion. His life has changed hugely in these past weeks, and it would be best if this final change—discovering he has a father after all—is absorbed into the overall changes to his life.'

He gave a final, long glance at her as she lay there, incapable of speech, reaction, and then without another word he was gone.

'Mummy, please may you cut a peach for me?'

Nicky selected the biggest one in the large blue pottery bowl on the table and handed it across to Rhianna with an expectant expression on his face.

She took it, and began to pare it with a knife. A fly buzzed idly in the lunchtime heat and she flicked it away. At the head of the table set on the wide terrace overlooking the beach Alexis Petrakis sat, relaxed back in his chair, half a glass of chilled Chablis in his hand.

Lunch had been a strange affair. Outwardly it had looked completely normal, with Nicky chattering away to both her and Alexis. All conversation had been centred on Nicky; hardly any direct exchanges between herself and Alexis had taken place. And when there had been one, always initiated by Alexis, never herself, he had been doggedly, scrupulously civil to her.

It had been totally unnerving.

Totally unreal.

A sense of complete weirdness enveloped Rhianna. It was as if all feeling, all thought, had been suspended. As if she had gone beyond emotion, beyond the will required for either function.

When Alexis had withdrawn from her bedroom, bombshell deposited, she had simply gone on staring at the space he had occupied, her mind groping flounderingly over what he had just said and done. Emotions like waves had come over her, each wave quite opposite from each other. One wave carried a surge of stunned, disbelief; the next surged with a kind of blind, inchoate fury that he should have dared to declare in so lordly a fashion that he now deigned to believe that she put her son at a higher value than his filthy money. But even after that wave had boiled through her, a third and final wave had taken its place. A sense of extreme and total exhaustion of the spirit. She just couldn't take any more.

And that was still with her as she sat opposite Alexis, cutting Nicky's peach for him, trying not to look anywhere near the tall, dark figure at the other end of the table, his saturnine face shaded by the overhang of the terrace roof.

'There you go, darling,' she said, pushing the prepared fruit towards Nicky.

He started to eat it with gusto, mumbling a 'thank you' as he did so, then, turning towards the end of the table, he said, 'Can we do more swimming after lunch? Please,' he added, then frowned, puzzled. 'Please, Mr—Mr Pe—Mr Petra—'

He stopped, not knowing how to continue.

Alexis set down his wine. 'You don't have to call me Mr Petrakis, Nicky,' he said.

And suddenly, quite suddenly, every nerve in Rhianna's body quivered. Desperately she tensed forward. But it was too late. Alexis was speaking again. His voice was careful, almost inexpressive, as if he were testing out each word for the weight it could bear.

'Nicky, tell me something. Did your mummy ever tell you about your daddy?'

The breath froze in Rhianna's throat. Oh, God, he's going to tell him now—right now. And I haven't had any time to prepare myself. Prepare Nicky…

'Nicky…' Her voice was faint.

Her son didn't hear her. Nicky was polishing off his peach. He looked across at the man who'd asked him the question.

'Mummy says I haven't got one. Not all children have daddies, she says.'

'Would you like one?'

There was reserve in Alexis's voice. It sounded quite neutral. In agony, Rhianna tried to catch his eye, to stop him. But she knew it was hopeless. He'd said he would tell Nicky and now it was happening.

Nicky frowned.

'Only if he's nice. Sometimes where we lived the daddies were not nice. They yelled and said rude words. Mummy used to go inside quickly and shut the door when they did that.'

Rhianna could see Alexis's face darken at Nicky's innocent depiction of the kind of environment he'd been brought up in.

'But if there was a nice daddy for you, who didn't yell, would you like that?'

'Would he be sick, like Grandpa?'

There was a note of fear in Nicky's voice, and Rhianna could see Alexis's mouth tighten, then deliberately relax again.

'No. He would be quite well. He could play football with you. And go swimming. Throw stones that bounce.'

Nicky's eyes widened. 'Like you can!'

Rhianna could see the set of Alexis's jaw tense.

'Yes, like I can. In fact…' The pause was minute, and for

a second Rhianna caught the unbearable tension in his voice, his face. 'Maybe I would make a good daddy.'

He sat still. Very, very still.

'Would I do, Nicky, for a daddy? If you wanted that?'

And suddenly, quite suddenly, out of nowhere, Rhianna felt tears prick in her eyes. She didn't want them there. Tried to stop them welling. But she couldn't stop them. Before her eyes, Nicky blurred.

'Just for on holidays? Like now?' There was caution in his voice.

'For as long as you'd want, Nicky. But we could start with now, couldn't we?'

For a long moment Nicky just stared. Then suddenly he had jumped to his feet. He came rushing round to Rhianna.

'Mummy! Can we? Can we have a daddy?'

His little hands clutched her arms; his face was alight. With eagerness, with questioning.

With hope.

Rhianna swallowed. Her eyes squeezed.

'If that's what you want, muffin, of course you can. Of course you…you can…'

Her voice choked. She didn't want to cry. Didn't want to cry because Alexis Petrakis was offering to be their son's father.

'Oh, Mummy!' Nicky's eyes were huge. 'We've got a daddy now! I've got a daddy!' He turned to the man who had made him so wonderful an offer. 'Can we start now? Please?'

Alexis nodded. 'Yes, we can start now.'

For a moment Rhianna saw through her blurred vision his mouth press tightly, his throat constrict.

Somehow it just made her vision blur even more.

CHAPTER NINE

'DADDY—come and see!'

'Daddy—look—look at me!'

'Daddy—watch! Daddy, watch!'

The refrains were constant, endless. Rhianna heard them all afternoon—Nicky's piping, excited voice, calling for his father. She lay on her day bed on the terrace, cool in the shade, propped up on pillows, completely inert. But, despite her physical inertia, mentally and emotionally she was a complete wreck. Tears kept filling her eyes, however much she tried to stop them, blink and brush them away. Just watching Nicky down on the beach, splashing in the sea, building a sandcastle, kicking a football around, the whole time his face a picture of ecstasy.

Once, during his play, he had suddenly stopped and rushed up to her, clambering up and hugging her so tightly that she could not breathe.

'Mummy! We've got a *daddy*! We've got a *daddy*!' Before rushing away again. Back to his Daddy.

Alexis Petrakis.

The man she had more cause to loathe in all the world than anyone else alive.

And yet…

How could she hate him now? How could she hate him now Nicky knew he was his father. Because if she did it would show. Nicky would find out. He'd feel her hatred, and it would be a poison for him…

Her thoughts were going round and round and round in her head as she sat and watched her son and his father playing, their figures blurring in and out of her vision.

119

But *could* she stop hating Alexis Petrakis? She'd hated him for five long draining, exhausting, gruelling years, when keeping going had been the only thing she could do—trying to keep her father alive, trying to give her baby the best she could, despite all the weight dragging her down, down, down...

Until she had finally collapsed.

And now her life had changed—changed completely.

Because of Alexis Petrakis.

What am I going to do? she thought. Her emotions felt as battered as if they had been shipwrecked, tossed in a tempestuous sea. But on what shore would they be cast up?

Tiredness seeped through her. She was too tired to think, too tired to feel. It was all too difficult, too confusing.

She would just go on lying here, in the warm sun, getting used to the fact that her son now knew he had a father—a father who wanted to be a permanent part of his life. For whose sake he was even prepared to be civil to his son's mother.

Her eyes rested on the pair of them, kicking a football back and forth towards makeshift goals marked by battered sand towers. Nicky was laughing and calling out, and Alexis—

There was a hollowing feeling inside her stomach. Out of nowhere it came, making her breath catch.

Alexis Petrakis—in casual chinos and polo shirt, his sable hair breeze-ruffled, his saturnine face animated with laughter.

The hollowing came again, making her feel suddenly weak and breathless.

She shut her eyes. Quite deliberately.

Alexis Petrakis existed only as Nicky's father. Nothing else.

Nothing else.

She had to remember that. She had to.

* * *

'Today,' announced Alexis, 'we are going on a boat. To a secret beach on the island.'

Nicky's eyes shone like stars as he lifted his head from his breakfast.

'A boat?' he echoed excitedly.

Alexis glanced at Rhianna. She had gone stark white, fear in her face.

'It is quite safe, and we will all wear lifejackets.'

'Mummy! *Please!*'

Every maternal instinct urged her to refuse. Boats went on the sea—the sea could drown children. But Nicky was looking so thrilled.

She took an uncertain breath. 'Well—I—I—'

'Yes, yes, yes!' Nicky bounced up and down in his seat.

'I am surprised you are so nervous about the sea,' Alexis commented. 'Considering your father designed yachts. Did you never go sailing with him as a child yourself?'

'I didn't see much of my father when I was growing up,' she answered shortly. 'My mother divorced him for desertion when I was not much older than Nicky. She lived in Oxfordshire, which is pretty far from the sea.'

She didn't want to talk about her childhood. And certainly not to Alexis Petrakis. But then she didn't want to talk to him at all. About anything.

Even though he kept on talking to her. He'd done it the previous day, with Nicky present, talking to her in a casual, conversational way—as if he had never thrown such vicious accusations at her, had never made her the target of his fury, his rage.

At least Nicky had been there as well, thankfully oblivious to the stiffness and undercurrents between the two people who had so unintentionally but so irrevocably brought him into existence. He had accepted his father's arrival in his life with a childish mix of unquestioning acceptance and thrilled excitement, as if Father Christmas had arrived.

She was less accepting. And in place of excitement was tension. Fraught, pulling tension, webbing her round.

She could not cope with Alexis being, as he had said he would be, 'civil' to her. Talking to her as if she were a normal human being, not excrement beneath his feet.

She could see it was an effort for him, though. That he was quite deliberately involving her in his conversation with Nicky, drawing her in.

But I don't want to be drawn in. I don't want to have anything to do with him.

Even as the words formed in her head she knew she could not indulge them. Loath as she was to acknowledge it, she knew that he was right. For Nicky's sake she must try and put aside her hostility—as he was doing.

But it was difficult to do so. Difficult to let go of something that had been there for five long years, like a caged beast—a beast that had been let terrifyingly loose when Alexis had turned up at her hospital bedside, and here, in his villa, when he had thrown his vileness at her.

Yet here she was, responding to his questions as if those vicious exchanges had never taken place.

A faint frown creased Alexis's brow.

'Your mother didn't like you spending time with your father?'

Was there something in his voice that had an edge to it?

'The other way round,' she replied defensively, not liking to hear her mother criticised. 'My father didn't have much time for me. Or for her. Or for anything, really, except his boats. So, no, I didn't sail as a child. I did a basic course on a reservoir, when I was a student, because I thought it would be something that would please my father, but—'

She fell silent. Why on earth was she telling this to Alexis Petrakis? Her pathetic attempts to get her father to take an interest in her.

'But?' His voice prompted her.

She gave a dismissive shrug of her shoulder.

'He didn't reply to my letter telling him I'd got my Level One dinghy certificate. So I never went any further with getting qualified.'

'What did you study as a student?'

Her eyes flickered to him. Why did he want to know?

'Accountancy. Very boring. But I knew it would make me employable. Mum never had much money—Dad was always late with his maintenance payments—so—'

'You are an accountant?'

There was surprise in his voice. She stared at him.

'Yes. After my mother died I sought out my father and went to work for him, to help keep his company going. I realised how bad the situation was financially, and knew the only way to save it was to find an investor or a buyer, or a part-owner. That's why I approached MML. I told you that.'

'You never told me you were an accountant.'

There was accusation in his voice. Her face hardened.

'What difference does it make what my professional qualifications were or are?' she retorted.

'Do you really need to ask?' he replied.

He was looking at her strangely.

With that same assessing look she caught on his face sometimes.

It disturbed her.

She got to her feet and held her hand out for Nicky.

'Time for teeth-brushing.'

He slid down from the table and went reluctantly with her.

The boat trip proved a huge thrill for Nicky. Wedged between his father's splayed legs, he gleefully steered the wheel, his hands shadowed by Alexis's. Seated in the stern, Rhianna hung on grimly, her body battered as the boat slapped over the waves.

But Nicky's joy and excitement made it worthwhile.

So did their destination.

It was indeed, a secret beach. Out at sea it was scarcely visible between two miniature headlands. But nestled between the cliffs was a tiny jewel-like beach, with dazzling white sand and exquisite shallow turquoise water.

'We're going to snorkel!' Nicky told her excitedly. 'Daddy and me!'

Alexis dropped anchor and jumped lithely overboard into knee deep water. He scooped Nicky up and deposited him on the beach a few yards away. Then he returned to the boat. He held out his arms to her.

'I can manage,' Rhianna said immediately. But as she got uncertainly to her feet the boat swung on its mooring. Instinctively she grasped the nearest solid object.

It was Alexis.

She clung, swaying, terrified. Then in a fluid movement he had scooped her up, as lightly as he had Nicky. For one fleeting moment she felt the protective strength of his arms.

Then she went completely rigid.

She'd frozen. As if she'd been turned into a block of wood.

Grimly, Alexis waded through the shallow water towards the tiny beach, the starkly rigid body immobile in his arms.

Thee mou, she hadn't been like this the night he had swept her up and carried her to his bed! Then she had been like warm honey in his arms, soft and pliant, yielding to him like sweetest velvet...

No—no point thinking of that. Remembering that. It was the last thing he wanted to recall to his mind.

And Rhianna Davies was the last woman on the planet he wanted to have the slightest sexual feeling about whatsoever. But for all that there was no reason for her freaking out whenever he touched her.

As if he were poison. Anathema to her.

He set her down on the sand and she jerked away from him immediately.

He busied himself carrying what they needed to shore and setting up a camp in the shade of the cliff. Nicky bounced around excitedly.

'Come on, Daddy!' He started rummaging through the grip containing snorkelling equipment.

'Steady,' said Alexis. 'Right—flippers first.'

Rhianna watched them from her position on a soft rug laid out on the sand. Her heart-rate was slowing again now. She'd discarded her lifejacket, but Alexis and Nicky still kept theirs on. Her eyes kept going to Alexis. Somehow the extra bulk over his chest simply made his shoulders seem broader in their short-sleeved T-shirt, his hips in their swimming shorts narrower, his bare, sinewed legs longer.

She felt that long-ago tremor start within her again.

Felt, for just a second, the echo of his protective clasp around her as he carried her ashore.

She shut her eyes.

A strange, vast and completely illogical sense of loss went through her. As though something very precious had gone from her life.

But that was stupid. She had never had Alexis Petrakis.

He had only had her—enjoyed her, and discarded her. He'd never intended anything more than a one-night stand. It had never meant more to him than that.

She must never forget that.

'Is he too heavy?'

Alexis nodded at Nicky, who—exhausted from the excitement of the boat trip and the exertions of snorkelling, then made soporific by Maria's lavish picnic lunch—was asleep on Rhianna's lap.

She shook her head. Alexis was lounging at the far end of

the rug with panther-like grace, his T-shirt moulding his physique, long bare legs extended, lithe and muscular, his feet bare.

She dragged her gaze away.

'He's never heavy.' She smiled, looking down at her sleeping son, love-light in her gaze. Her hand smoothed over the silky hair.

Something flickered in Alexis's eyes.

Her smile did something to her. It lightened her face. Softened it. He found himself studying her as she gazed down at Nicky. Not that it was haggard any more. That hollowed-out gauntness she'd had was completely gone. Now she simply looked fine-boned, not thin. Nor did her skin look like sickly sour cheese any more. The warmth of the Mediterranean sun had brought a honeyed tone to her face. The bright Aegean sky had made her eyes bluer, too, not washed-out.

In fact—

He halted his mental catalogue. Rhianna Davies's physical appearance was completely irrelevant. She was his son's mother. Nothing more.

And an accountant?

His brows drew together in a frown. Had she really been her father's accountant that night she'd said she'd wanted to talk to him privately?

I could check. There are records of those who have professional qualifications.

Because if she truly were, then maybe, just maybe, her claim of innocence of the accusation he'd charged her with was wrong.

And if that was wrong—

Again he halted himself.

No. Even if she hadn't deliberately offered herself to him on a plate, to soften him up to plead her case over her father's company, it did not exonerate her! She was *still* guilty of keeping Nicky from him—deliberately and knowingly keeping a son from his father.

Cruel, vindictive, vengeful.

His mouth thinned. Why did that sound so familiar...?

'Tell me what he was like as a baby. Do you have any photos?'

Rhianna's eyes lifted again. There was a curious expression on Alexis's face. Reserved, almost shuttered. Yet there was something else there too. It was hunger, she realised. Something pricked inside her, and she realised what it was.

Guilt.

Guilt that he had never seen his child as a baby. That those lost years would never come back for him.

A hollowness opened inside her, filled with stabbing pain. Loss.

'Some,' she answered, feeling awkward. It was hard enough speaking to him when Nicky was present. Now, with him asleep in her lap, and it was only her and Alexis, and it was even harder.

'I—I would like to see them some time.'

Had he sounded hesitant? Alexis Petrakis? Rich, powerful, domineering, demanding Alexis Petrakis? A man who simply clicked his fingers and things happened the way he wanted them? A man who felt he could throw the most foul insults in her face and they were justified?

A man who had no memories of his baby son...

'They're...they're in my flat. I haven't got many, though. He...he was a very good baby.' She paused. 'That sounds terrible. It usually means placid—no trouble. He wasn't any trouble. I was—' she caught her breath '—very grateful. My father...' She swallowed. 'Well, he wasn't well—I made allowances. I had to.' She shrugged.

'Did he resent Nicky?'

She looked away, out over the azure water that was a million miles away from the cramped, poky flat on the run-down housing estate where she and Nicky and her father had lived.

'Yes,' she answered briefly, and she did not hear the edge of bitterness in her voice as she spoke. 'My father resented anything and anyone that came between him and his work.'

'Do you miss him?'

Her lips pressed together.

'No. It's an awful thing to say, but I don't. He didn't care about my mother, or about me, or about his grandchild. So why should anyone care about him? I—I did my best for him. It was all I could do. But it was never enough. I could never get back for him the one thing he loved—his company. And so after a while—eventually—I stopped caring that he didn't care. I had Nicky and that was enough. More than enough.' Her voice lowered. 'He was everything—everything to me. And he still is. And he always will be.'

Her jaw tightened, defiance in her eyes. 'Nicky's happiness is the only, *only* reason I am here now. You've made Nicky happy—'

Her voice broke off. There was a long, constrained moment, then abruptly Alexis spoke.

'Why did you cry when I told him I was his father?'

She pressed her lips together again.

'I was happy for him. You've—you've—' She took a deep breath, lifted her chin, then said what she knew she had to say. 'You've done well by him. I—I was surprised. You really do seem to…to want him, to care for him.'

Alexis spoke slowly, his eyes not quite meeting hers. 'Why did you think I would not? Did you think—' his eyes suddenly went back to hers '—that I would be like your father?'

There was a heaviness, sudden, crushing, in the air.

She swallowed, her throat felt dry.

'I—I—' She closed her eyes. 'Yes.'

Alexis looked at her. For a long, long moment he said nothing. Then quietly, very quietly, he spoke.

'I will love Nicky with all my heart, with all my soul, with all my being, until the day I die. When I first set eyes on him and knew him for my son I knew that I would never, *never* reject him. As—as my own father had rejected me.'

She stared at him, her face stilling. His eyes were holding hers steadily, unflinchingly.

'You see, like you,' he said, in that same quiet, steady voice, 'I spent my childhood, my adolescence, wanting my father to love me. But he never did.' He took a breath, his voice changing. 'He never did.'

She heard the tightening in his voice, and without conscious thought, only impelled by an instinct it was impossible to suppress, she suddenly reached forward and touched—oh, so lightly; oh, so briefly—his hand, splayed on the rug, taking his lounging weight. She drew back immediately, but it was done.

Between them, for the briefest moment, there flowed something that brought them together. Two people whose childhoods had been blighted by the cruelty of adults.

And suddenly—quite, quite suddenly—Rhianna knew with a certainty that filled her being that Nicky was safe—safe with the man who had fathered him, who would never, never betray a child's love.

She felt the tears prick in her eyes.

'We can do this. We can do this, Rhianna.' Alexis's voice was low, steady and compelling. 'We can be good parents for Nicky—the kind of parents every child needs. Loving parents. We both love him, and for his sake we can do this.'

He didn't say what 'this' was, but he did not have to. Rhianna knew.

'This' was what he had asked her to do—put aside their hatred and mistrust of each other just enough for Nicky's sake.

Emotions sifted through her like sediments shifting, finding new levels.

Cautiously, very cautiously, she answered him, feeling her chest tighten.

'I—I will try,' she said.

He nodded. His eyes still held hers.

'Thank you,' he said quietly.

It was late afternoon before they returned to the villa. Nicky had awoken, refreshed and eager for more snorkelling, more swimming and a lot of exploring of the rocks and beach with his father. Rhianna had watched them. Something had changed, she knew. Something about the way she thought of Alexis.

Knowing that his childhood had been blighted, as hers had been, had done more than explain to her why he was so determined to be a good father to Nicky—it had made him somehow more human. Not just a rich, powerful man, using his wealth to bully or buy others, but vulnerable. Human.

Not the way she had had cause to think of him for five long years.

But now?

Her mood was strange as they arrived back. Nicky went rushing off to find Karen and extol the wonders of his day to her over nursery tea, Alexis went off to shower and then go into his office, and Rhianna surrendered to Nurse Thompson's ministrations.

She took her medicines and did her physio exercises docilely, but her mood was abstracted. So abstracted that as she sat at her dressing table after her bath, and Nurse Thompson set to drying her newly washed hair, she was taken aback, when the hairdryer was finally silenced, by the reflection that looked back at her from the mirror.

'Good heavens!' she exclaimed faintly.

Nurse Thompson had blowdried her hair as skilfully as if she'd been a professional hairdresser. Not that she'd been to a hairdresser for five years, Rhianna thought. It was a luxury she hadn't been able to afford, and, given her utterly absent social life, not something she'd needed.

Not that she needed it now, either. But Nurse Thompson was standing behind her, looking so pleased with her efforts that Rhianna hadn't the heart to say anything other than, 'It looks wonderful!'

And it did.

Her hair, just skimming her shoulders, flicked inwards, lifting her brow, setting off her face in a way that reminded her, with a strange, yearning pang, of how she had once looked many long years ago.

Nurse Thompson smiled, satisfied. 'Make-up next.'

On cue, Karen walked in with a make-up bag.

'What's going on?' Rhianna asked, bemused.

'Nurse Thompson says patients get better faster when they know they look nice. Psycho-whatsit, but it works,' said Karen cheerfully.

'Quite right,' said Nurse Thompson. 'Now, just sit still. Consider it part of your convalescence.'

Rhianna gave in. She let Karen make up her face, lend her a brightly patterned red and yellow summer dress, put a string of beads around her neck and squeeze her feet into a pair of her sandals.

At the end of it all, Karen stood back.

'Wow!' she announced. 'You look fantastic!'

Behind her, Nurse Thompson nodded approvingly.

'Yes, indeed,' she agreed. 'No one would ever think you'd been ill!'

Rhianna stared. No, she thought slowly. She did not look ill any more. What she looked was—

Like I used to look.

She stared wonderingly. For five years her appearance had been something of total irrelevance to her.

It still is.

The words thudded in her head. They were joined by more, thudding just as heavily.

You don't have anyone to look good for. No one.

And especially not Alexis Petrakis. He's Nicky's father— that's all he is to you. All. Remember that.

She took the self-admonishment unflinchingly. After all, it was only the truth.

But her changed appearance did not pass unnoticed by Nicky. As she went in to kiss him goodnight his eyes widened.

'Mummy! You look beautiful!'

She gave a smile. 'Thank you, my darling.'

He held out his arms to her.

'Need a kiss,' he said.

Rhianna obliged, wrapping him up tight in her arms.

'I can only blow a kiss,' she said, holding him back a little. 'Or I'll get lipstick on you.'

Nicky kissed her instead, smacking kisses on each cheek.

'Mummy,' he said in a satisfied voice, and lay back again. He snuggled into the pillow. 'Mummy, Nicky, Daddy,' he announced. 'And Teddy.' He hugged the battered bear close to him.

'Daddy has said goodnight already,' he informed her. 'He said we could go on the boat again tomorrow. He said I could drive again. He said…' His voice started to fade.

Rhianna sat beside him, holding his hand as he drifted off to sleep. Then she reached and clicked off the bedside light, leaving the nightlight glowing in the dimness. For a long moment she just went on sitting there, her hand touching his, feeling endless love for her son just pouring and pouring out of her, like a bottomless blessing. Then, at length, she leant forward to bestow a last, light air-kiss on Nicky's brow, stood up, and turned to go.

And stopped dead.

Alexis was standing in the open doorway to the hallway.

The light behind him made him look darker, but there was something about his stillness that made her freeze.

Then he stood to one side, holding the door back for her.

Feeling incredibly, ridiculously self-conscious, she walked towards him, squeezing past him to gain the hall. How long had he been there? Since before she'd turned the bedside light out?

As she reached the hall she paused, and half turned. What she wanted to do was go off and find Nurse Thompson and Karen and share whatever meal they were having. It was what—blessedly—she'd done the evening before. She'd had tea with Nicky and his father, but then Alexis had disappeared off into his office— presumably to pay attention to his business empire via his PC and telephone. Rhianna had helped Karen put Nicky to bed, and afterwards had eaten with her and Nurse Thompson.

Neither, she'd noticed, had made the slightest reference to the fact that their employer was now openly acknowledging that Nicky was his son. Well, Rhianna had thought, they were good, discreet staff who mutely accepted whatever happened in the rich households they worked in.

The household staff behaved with similar discretion, and now, as Stavros emerged from the kitchen regions and came to hold open the door at the dining room side of the hall, he simply murmured, '*Kyria…*' in his usual polite tone.

Inside the dining room Rhianna could see that the table had been laid for only two. Instant recollection of the last meal she'd eaten in here rushed back at her—the ugly scene that had sent her running from the room.

But she had to put that behind her. Strive with all her effort for the rapprochement that Alexis wanted. Not for her sake, but for their son's.

And for Nicky's sake she would have to comply.

She took the chair Stavros was holding out for her. Alexis

took his place opposite her. As she settled herself, her eyes flicked across the table.

He was staring at her, transfixed.

It was the past come to life. Alexis's eyes worked over Rhianna as she sat there, a few feet away. Shock ricocheted through him.

Yes, she was five years older, in her late twenties, not her early twenties, and her hair was shorter, her face thinner.

But still quite, quite stunning.

And wearing at last, he registered, something that did not look as if it had been thrown away on a rubbish tip. The dress was only a chainstore garment, but it was a universe away from the faded T-shirts and worn, baggy cotton trousers that she'd worn till now.

The dress even showed that she still possessed breasts...

His eyes flickered over the two delineated mounds. The neckline might be modest, but the material of the bodice curved lovingly.

Enticingly.

A long, slow pulse began to beat in his veins.

Rhianna had to steel herself to keep still. She wanted to leap to her feet and run. Bolt.

His intense look was excruciating. She didn't know where to look, what to do.

Damn Nurse Thompson and Karen! What on earth have they done?

But she knew exactly what they'd done. They'd turned her back into a woman. She hadn't been that for a long, long time.

Not for five years.

Not since Alexis Petrakis had peeled the clothes from her body and laid her down upon his bed...

Memory leapt in her, like a flame from a dead fire that someone had just thrown petrol on.

She couldn't stop it. Couldn't douse it.

Her eyes met the dark obsidian eyes across the table. Met and leapt.

Memory drenched her. Memory of those eyes looking down at her, drowning her in their depths, their desire…

It was alive again—that overpowering, devastating, *shameful* desire. The way it had leapt between them that evening five long, long years ago. She tried to force it back, thrust it away, hammer it back down deep, deep, where it could not escape.

But it came all the same, and she could not stop it—was helpless, formless, shapeless. She was liquid, rich, slow-pouring honey that creamed like velvet through her veins.

I don't want to feel this. I don't want to! I don't want to want him!

Words seared in her mind—poisonous, powerful.

But you do want him. You want him as much now as you wanted him then…

The terrible damning truth hollowed through her.

You will never be able to resist him…

Never.

Despair flooded through her. Despair and a churning dismay. She had to fight what she was feeling—she had to! She must not succumb to something that had damaged her so badly, so irretrievably. Summoning all her strength, she banished by sheer force of will the debilitating weakness that flooded through her.

Her chin lifted, her chest rising and falling as she fought to regain her composure, fought to be the person she knew she *must* be.

Nicky's mother. Nothing more.

Just as she was nothing more to Alexis Petrakis.

Gratefully she seized the glass of white wine Stavros had

poured for her. She took a sip, feeling its reviving strength. Tonight she needed it.

She wanted to run, fly. But even to do that would be to acknowledge what was happening, to give credence to the reason why Alexis Petrakis was sitting opposite her, his eyes fixed on her.

She wouldn't—she wouldn't do it.

So she had to say something—anything that sounded normal.

She said the first thing that came into her head.

'Thank you for taking Nicky for the boat trip. He absolutely adored it.'

For a second Alexis made no response. Then, with a visible effort, he replied. 'But it was too rough for you. Tomorrow I'll take you out sailing. See how much you remember from your dinghy course.'

'Almost nothing,' she said hurriedly.

'Well, we shall see. And with a light wind it will be much gentler for you,' Alexis returned.

Stavros arrived with the first course—an *assiette* of seafood. It was a welcome diversion. By the time she had helped herself to what she wanted, and Alexis had done similarly, her composure was recovering.

So, it seemed, was Alexis's. Yet even as the pair of them determinedly made civil conversation across the dinner table—first about sailing in general, and then, with Alexis taking the lead, about the particular maritime conditions of the Aegean: the prevailing northerly *meltemi* of the summer, the sudden squalls, the complicated shifting local currents of this tideless sea—she felt, beneath her skin, that he was only half concentrating on what he was saying. There was a subtle but discernible air of abstraction about him.

It disturbed her, but she did not know why.

She had no spare energy to wonder about it. She needed all she had simply to keep going, having what on the outside seemed a normal conversation with Alexis Petrakis. Doggedly, she laboured away—asking questions, responding when appropriate—as if he were simply a social acquaintance. They didn't even talk about Nicky

Yet if Nicky did not exist they would not be sitting here, opposite each other, trying to talk politely to each other. And it was for his sake that she had to make an effort, she knew. Force herself to be 'normal' with him—as if he really were just a social acquaintance. The more she did it, the easier it would get, she told herself.

And at least, she registered gratefully, he had stopped staring at her.

It was just the shock. That's all. Seeing me look so different. That's why he stared.

And she must be glad that it was so—very glad.

Very glad indeed. Relieved.

Grateful, in fact.

She took a breath and asked another question about sailing.

When the meal finally reached the coffee stage she was even more grateful. The strain had begun to tell. Emotions were running in her, beneath the surface. She did not know what they were, but they were swelling, growing. She'd kept the promise that she had given Alexis that afternoon, that she would try to make this rapprochement work.

But though she knew now that Nicky was safe with Alexis, that he was bound to his son by the strongest of emotional ties, there was one thing she must remember—one question she could not answer.

This civility from him was not for her sake, but for Nicky's. And though she could trust him with Nicky, after all the foulness that had passed between them, could *she* ever be safe with Alexis? Could she trust him to trust *her*?

She did not have long to wait to find out.

* * *

They took coffee on the terrace.

It was a lovely evening—the mildest yet, she thought. From the bushes came the constant, invisible soft chirruping of the cicadas. A soft zephyr winnowed the water, which shushed on the sand in a gentle murmur. Stavros had placed a candle on the table, along with the coffee tray, and beyond its little pool of light the darkness draped itself across the terrace in a velvet fall, softened only by the dim moonlight playing on the silvery sand and the night-lit sea.

'Are you cold?' Alexis asked her.

She shook her head.

'No. Thank you. I'm fine. This is lovely.'

She relapsed into silence, letting her eyes become dark-adjusted. Across the table Alexis's dark bulk took shape, his long-sleeved, open-necked white shirt reflecting the pale moonlight, though his face was in shadow.

She took a slow sip of coffee, inhaling the distinctive fragrance. From the corner of her eye, as she looked out over the night-dark sand and sea, she could see Alexis lean back, stretching out his long legs under the table and cupping his glass of ouzo in his hands, his tiny cup of Greek coffee as yet untouched. Like her, he seemed content to sit in silence. She went on looking at how the moonlight caught the white caps of the tiny waves as they crested in miniature surf on the beach.

No sound came from the rest of the villa. The staff quarters were on the side away from the beach, she knew, and Nicky was fast asleep.

It was a peaceful scene. Yet beneath the tranquil surface deep currents ran.

Her thoughts ran on down twisting paths, uncertain ways.

The future stretched before her like the night over the sea. An impenetrable veil.

What was going to happen? Not now, here on this peaceful island, but when she was well again. What was going to happen to her and Nicky? Alexis had threatened so much—yet now he wanted a kind of peace between them.

So did he trust her now? Trust her to be a fit mother for his son?

She felt the currents shift and stir within her. Uncertainty hemmed her in.

She let her eyes go back to him. Her expression was troubled. Guarded.

His was—unreadable.

But as she studied his face he said quietly, 'What is it?'

'What's going to happen?' she asked. Her voice was troubled. 'You said you wanted rapprochement—enough peace between us for Nicky not to be damaged by the lack of it. But what happens next?'

She searched his face, as if trying to see behind the veil of his eyes.

For one long moment he looked at her. She could not read his expression. Perhaps, she realised, it was because there was no expression to read. And yet somewhere deep she could sense tension running through him.

Then he spoke.

'What happens next?' he echoed, his deep voice low. 'I think there is only one answer to that.'

He let his eyes rest on her.

'We get married,' he said.

CHAPTER TEN

FOR a moment Rhianna just went on staring. It was as if her brain were moving in slow motion, unable to catch up with what she had just heard. Had she heard it? *Had* she really just heard Alexis Petrakis say that?

Her mouth opened.

'Get married?' she echoed dumbly.

He inclined his head. 'It is,' he said, 'the obvious thing to do. Nicky needs two parents. Normal parents. Stability. A family. So we get married.'

She stared at him.

'You're mad,' she said.

Something moved in his eyes, but it was not anger.

'Think about it,' he said, and took a mouthful of ouzo.

'*Think* about it? I don't need to think about it!' Her voice had risen in pitch. She could feel adrenaline starting to pump round her body. 'This is some kind of joke, right? Some kind of tasteless, ludicrous joke that…that…'

Words failed her.

'I repeat—it's the obvious thing to do.' He seemed supremely untroubled by her vehement reaction. But deep in his eyes his expression was hidden. 'We both want Nicky and Nicky needs both of us—full-time parents, who live in the same place, who make a family for him, a home. Wherever we are in the world he is with both of us, and we both have him.'

Rhianna placed her hands flat on the table. 'Stop it,' she said. 'Stop it! This is just stupid and tasteless and absurd and…and… Good God, I've never heard anything so *insane* in my life!'

That flicker, deep in his eyes, came again.

140

'Would you care to tell me why?'

There was an edge in his voice now, she heard. Not much, for him, but it was there.

She just stared at him still.

'Why? You ask *why*? After everything you've called me? Everything you've done to me? You've tried to take Nicky from me. Again and again. First you tried to bully me into it, threatening me and reviling me, and then you tried to *buy* him from me with your filthy money!'

'I told you—I had to check what kind of woman you were.' His tone was dismissive. 'Whether you were after my money and were using my son to get it. When you turned down twenty million pounds for him then I knew—knew that Nicky was safe with you. Rhianna—' His voice had changed abruptly. 'This is not necessary. I have accepted that you are not the kind of woman I thought you were when I discovered Nicky's existence. We have moved on from there. You do not have to prove to me that you are not a gold-digger.'

Her eyes flashed.

'Just someone who thought she could sweeten you up for a company takeover by going to bed with you?'

Venom bit in her words.

She saw his face tense for a moment, then, deliberately, he said, 'We have moved on from there as well.'

Rhianna leant forward in her chair. 'Have we? Have we really?'

'Yes. Confirmation from the UK of both your qualifications as an accountant and your position as your father's company accountant five years ago were waiting for me when we came back from our boat trip today.'

'You went and checked that out?' she asked slowly.

'Yes. And understanding, as I now do, the pressure you were under—your father being dangerously ill, your difficult relationship with him, the urgent need to get the go-ahead on the takeover—I can appreciate how you thought it necessary to approach me in the way you did at that dinner. Striking up a—rapport—with me, coming back up to my room so promptly. Even though—' his voice changed minutely '—such an approach was open to misinterpretation by me.'

'Misinterpretation.' Her voice was hollow.

She could feel hysteria beading in her. Misinterpretation. That was all it was, was it?

He was speaking again, cutting through the emotion welling up in her inexorably.

'So, yes, we can now—both of us—move on. Think about the future. Nicky's future. We both accept that that is the only important thing. For him to be happy. That is why it would be best for him if we married. To give him security, stability, a home, a family—that is what he needs.'

Emotions churned in her. Swirled like a dark tide. His face was impassive, unreadable, but there was something—something about it she could almost read in his opaque night-dark eyes.

And then suddenly she knew what it was. Out of nowhere, like a sharp gust of wind biting through her, she knew what this was all about.

'My, God,' she breathed. 'I know what you're doing. You gave yourself away when you said you had to check what sort of woman I was. This is another one of your tests—isn't it? *Isn't it?* You're dangling the prospect of marriage to you in front of my nose. And if I snap it up then you'll know you were right all along—that I really *am* a gold-digger! That I just *love* the idea of being a millionaire's wife! Absolutely *adore* it! Swanning around in designer clothes and diamonds for the rest of my life! A real, live gold-digger who's not fit to look after her son!'

The breath hissed in her throat.

'Well, you can just go to hell!'

She started to push her chair back, stumbling to her feet.

'Rhianna—that is *not* why I said we should get married!'

'It's *exactly* why you said it! It's another of your bloody tests. Well, I'm not having it—do you hear me?'

She lifted up her arm and brought it in a jerking, slashing, slanting movement downwards.

'No more,' she said. 'No. More.'

Something rolled through her like a huge, unstoppable wave.

It should have been anger.

But it was not.

It was hurt.

She shut her eyes. Why should she be feeling hurt? Hadn't she faced up to the question of whether Alexis trusted her with Nicky? Hadn't she been filled with doubt? With caution?

So why, now that she had her answer—had it clear and loud—did it *hurt*?

She had made the worst mistake of all. She had lowered her guard. Believed him. *Trusted him*. Trusted him when he'd talked of rapprochement, trusted him when he'd talked of making peace between them for their son's sake. Trusted him when he'd told her why she could be sure that he would always love his son as his father had never loved him. That he was fit to be Nicky's father.

But he hadn't trusted *her*. He hadn't trusted her to be fit to be Nicky's mother.

She turned away, opening her eyes, stumbling along the terrace. Her eyes were blurring, stinging, and she hated herself for it.

'Rhianna—'

She heard his chair scrape, and rapid footsteps.

Her arm was taken.

'Let me go! I don't want you touching me. I don't want your hands on me!' She spoke with dull vehemence. 'Never again. Never, ever again.'

She shook him loose, still not looking at him, making her way slowly around the corner of the terrace to where it passed by the front of her bedroom.

He didn't come after her. The French windows were unlocked, and she went inside.

Shutting out Alexis Petrakis.

Hell and damnation. Alexis's mouth tightened.

How in God's name had he mishandled that so badly?

Sending her bolting into hiding from him again.

Grimly he strode back to the table and threw himself in his chair, reaching for the ouzo bottle and pouring himself a generous second measure.

The strong liquorice-scented liquor burned down his throat as he swallowed it.

How had he made such a crass mistake? Blurting out an offer of marriage like that.

The moment the words had come out of his mouth he'd known he'd made a major error. But then he'd hardly been thinking straight all through the meal.

When have I ever thought straight around Rhianna Davies?

He hadn't the first night he'd met her, when her beauty had totally knocked him him out, and he hadn't tonight.

He'd got through the meal somehow, but it had been hard. All he'd wanted to do was sit and look at her. Drink her in.

Thee mou, but she was so beautiful!

He stared out into the darkness. The moon had scudded behind clouds. The night was thick, impenetrable. All he could hear was the soft sound of the waves and the cicadas.

And the slow beat of his pulse.

I want her again.

I wanted her from the first moment I laid eyes on her.

And I want her again.

He felt his body stir.

He reached for his ouzo, taking a slow mouthful. The fiery spirit burned in his throat. Just as his body was starting to burn.

Burn for the woman he desired.

But who did not desire him.

Who flinched away from him. Who yelled at him never to touch her again.

His eyes narrowed as he set back his glass.

Well, he would not be deterred by her revulsion to his touch. He had made Rhianna Davies quicken with desire for him before. Made her melt for him in his arms.

He would do so again.

But it would be a delicate operation. A very delicate operation. He would have to proceed very, very carefully. He could afford to make no more errors such as he'd made tonight.

But he would succeed.

Too much was at stake for him not to.

CHAPTER ELEVEN

'YOU see? I told you Dr Paniotis would be pleased with your progress.'

Nurse Thompson's voice was a mix of reassurance and satisfaction.

Rhianna smiled faintly. Overhead she could hear the thud-thud-thud of the helicopter carrying the doctor back to the mainland. She knew she should be as pleased as Nurse Thompson expected her to be. Her strength was coming back, she felt better, fitter, her drug dosages were declining all the time.

But depression filled her. It had done so all night, all morning—a dull, pressing heaviness that not even Nicky's cheerfulness could assuage. She knew what had caused it.

Alexis. Alexis Petrakis.

Still distrusting of her, still thinking the worst of her. Still wanting to prove that she was as bad as he so obviously wanted her to be...

Still unfit to be his son's mother.

She tried to summon anger, the anger that had fuelled her resistance to him all this time, but it would not come.

Instead, she found she simply wanted to cry.

'Now, a nice cup of tea for you, and then we can get you dressed.'

Nurse Thompson's brisk cheer grated this morning. Rhianna nodded dully. She had not got up yet, had waited for the doctor to complete his examination. Karen had whisked Nicky off, and Alexis was apparently immersed in his office, had been since early morning. She had not set eyes on him.

Murmuring a listless thank you, she took the cup of tea

that Nurse Thompson was handing to her. As she sipped, she heard footsteps and muffled voices outside her door. There was some scuffling and giggling, and then a very loud, rapid knocking.

Nurse Thompson walked across to the bedroom door and opened it.

A huge bouquet of flowers advanced into the room.

'Goodness me!' exclaimed the nurse. 'Walking flowers? Whatever next!'

Gleeful childish laughter sounded from behind the bouquet.

'It's me! It's me!' Nicky cried out, and lowered the flowers sufficiently to show his face. 'Mummy, Mummy—these are for you! Daddy said!'

He marched up to the bed and deposited a mass of flowers, swathed in cellophane and ribbons, on Rhianna's lap.

Her eyes went from the flowers to her son's grinning face, and then to the tall shape standing in the doorway.

'Do you like them, Mummy? Do you? They came in the helicopter! All the way from the city! Daddy said!'

'They're beautiful,' she told him. Her emotions were a confused tangle, knotting themselves around her. 'Thank you.' She reached to kiss him.

'They're from me *and* Daddy,' Nicky informed her.

'The card is from me.'

Alexis's voice from the doorway was low-pitched, yet it seemed to do something strange to Rhianna's insides. Her eyes slipped to the card tucked into the binding ribbon. She picked it up and opened it.

Please forgive me. Alexis.

She stared, disbelievingly. Then her gaze flew to him.

He started to walk towards her. His eyes were holding hers, and in them, she saw—even more disbelievingly—was an expression that she had never thought to see in his eyes.

Contrition.

He came and stood by the end of the bed. She stared at him, then her gaze was diverted. Stavros was entering with an armful of flat boxes. Nurse Thompson hurried to help him deposit them on a hastily drawn up chair.

'Mummy! Mummy! There are *more* presents! Lots more! Can I help you open them? Please, please?'

Nicky was bouncing with excitement.

Her emotions were still churning like a concrete mixer, but she could not refuse her son. She nodded, and immediately he fell upon the topmost box, yanking off the lid. As he did so, his little face fell.

'It's just clothes,' he said disgustedly.

'Your mother will like them,' said Alexis. His eyes moved to Rhianna. 'At least, I hope you will.'

Again there was that speaking look in his eyes, and again Rhianna just gazed at him.

Nicky was pulling out carefully folded garments interlined with tissue paper. They had clearly come from an expensive shop.

'I'll just pop these into water,' announced Nurse Thompson, and relieved Rhianna of the bouquet, disappearing with Stavros out into the hall.

Rhianna was left with Nicky and his father, and a lot of clothes-boxes.

And a lot of clothes.

Beautiful clothes. Beach clothes in vibrant colours—casually styled but, she could see immediately, beautifully and expensively made. The kind of beach clothes the women in Alexis's world wore. A universe away from the charity shop cast-offs that her wardrobe consisted of.

She stared, bemused, as Nicky riffled through the boxes, dumping clothes haphazardly on the bed. Alexis watched, with half an amused eye on Nicky and with half a quite different eye on Rhianna.

'Do you like them?' he asked. 'Karen told me your size,

and I had a stylist select them and flew them in. But if they are not to your taste they can be changed for others.'

'I can't accept them.'

Her voice was blunt.

He frowned.

'Why do you say that?'

'Why do you think?' she retorted tightly.

A little hand was tugging at her hand.

'Mummy, don't you like them?'

Nicky's voice sounded anxious. Alexis interceded smoothly.

'Your mother thinks I should not give her clothes. I think that's silly, don't you? I think daddies should give mummies clothes and presents and things. Don't you?'

Leave Nicky out of this! Rhianna wanted to shout. But it was too late. Nicky was nodding vigorously.

'I like this one best,' he said, and picked up a royal blue top with a beautiful appliqué design on it. 'I like blue,' he said wistfully.

'Do you? Hmm…I wonder…'

Suddenly Alexis was stooping down, lifting up another two boxes. These were not tastefully decorated with stylish logos. They were boldly patterned with animal shapes.

'Have a look in here,' said Alexis.

Nicky ripped off the lid.

'These are for me!' he announced breathlessly, and he held up a shorts and T-shirt outfit in his size, the shorts bright blue and the top blue and white striped, with a sailing boat on it. Then he dived into the box to discover the rest folded beneath.

'We've *both* got new clothes!' he said, eyes shining, to Rhianna.

'Holiday clothes,' said Alexis. 'For while you are here on holiday.'

Oh, cunning, thought Rhianna bitterly. Nicky was already pulling off his faded charity-shop T-shirt and yanking the expensive new one over his head. Alexis helped him, and then helped him change into the matching shorts.

'Very smart,' he said approvingly.

Nicky's eyes shone.

'These are the *best* clothes I've ever had!' he announced. 'Do I look smart, Mummy? Daddy says I do.'

'Very smart,' she agreed, fighting to hide her emotions from him. 'Why not go and show Karen?'

She could be cunning too, she thought sourly.

He hared off, and when he was gone Rhianna turned on Alexis.

'What is this?' she demanded. 'Another test?' Her voice was scathing, vicious. 'Well, you can take these clothes and—'

Alexis's hand flew up.

'No!' Then, in a milder tone, he said, 'I bought them for you because—because I thought you would like them.'

'I don't want clothes from you! I don't want anything from you!'

Her voice had risen in pitch, colour flaring along her cheeks.

Something shifted in his face. Fleetingly. Swiftly masked.

Then, without invitation, he sat himself down on the bed. Instantly she shifted her legs sideways. It was a huge double bed, but she could feel the weight of his mass depressing the mattress.

She could not understand why, but it felt, acutely, a very intimate gesture. Alexis Petrakis. Sitting on her bed.

She felt her breath catch, her stomach jitter.

'Please—do not flinch away from me.' There was a tightness in his voice. He took a swift breath. 'Rhianna, listen to me—for just a few moments, that is all. I should never have said what I did last night. But believe this of me: I was not, you have my word, seeking to test you again. I was thinking of Nicky, that was all. Nothing more. But there is no rush to make decisions of any kind. Nicky is only just getting used to the changes in his life. Let him do so at his own pace. And *you* do so at yours.'

He got to his feet.

'I will call Nurse Thompson for you. Please take the clothes, Rhianna. They are a gesture—nothing more. Besides—' his mouth twisted '—I think Nicky will be upset if you do not wear them. It will make him feel awkward about wearing the ones he has got. And he needed new clothes, Rhianna—even you must admit that!'

He picked up a sundress, half hidden under a pair of culottes. It was a creamy blonde colour, with tiny shoestring straps.

'This matches your hair,' he said softly.

He looked down at her.

Rhianna felt her heart begin to quicken. The way he was looking at her…almost smiling, not quite, but holding her eyes, just holding them…

Then he released her.

He replaced the sundress. When he spoke again his voice was very different.

'Are you happy if I take Nicky swimming now? The helicopter also delivered some pool toys for him, which I am sure he will enjoy.'

She swallowed. 'You don't have to ask me,' she said. She felt a swirling inside her, a confusion of emotion. 'He adores going swimming with you.'

'It is a pleasure for me too,' he answered. There was an emotion in his voice she would have been deaf not to hear. 'And I thank God that with him, at least, I do not seem to have made mistakes. But with you…' His eyes were dark and depthless, and she felt a strange disturbing pull inside her. 'With you I have made too many mistakes. I don't want to make a single one more.' There was an intensity about the way he was looking at her. 'Believe me.'

He took his leave and she went on sitting there, confusion

lacing and unlacing through her. She tried to make sense of what had just happened.

Alexis Petrakis being *nice* to her?

Apologising to her?

Asking her to believe him...

She lay back, bemused. Confused.

Can I trust him? This time can I really trust him?

The question tormented her.

Because she could find no answer.

And yet it seemed, over the next days, that he was answering her question all the time.

He was being so *nice* to her—so incredibly nice.

It was as if he were a different person.

The person he was with Nicky.

Smiling, open, spontaneous.

At first it made her feel awkward, gauche, tense. She found she kept looking out for the mask to slip, for the real Alexis Petrakis to break out again.

But it never did.

It was as if the foul, ugly words he had thrown at her had never been voiced. As if he had never accused her of any of the crimes he had laid at her feet.

And slowly, day by day, she found the words growing dimmer, fading away. Because how could she keep in her head the litany of his harsh and unjust accusations when he was behaving to her as if she were a different person from the one he had condemned as an unfit mother? When day after day he did nothing but treat her with kid gloves, drawing her in, making her part of the relationship he was building, stronger and more secure with every passing hour, with Nicky?

And so little by little she found that she was doing something she had never thought possible. She was coming to trust him. To feel—safe—with him.

It was easiest still, she acknowledged, to do so in Nicky's

company. Whether they were eating together, or out on the water in the dinghy or the motor boat, or in the pool, or on the beach, or seated at the table on the terrace playing board games and cards—Nicky ecstatic when he won, disgusted when he lost—or reading to him in bed when he was drifting off to sleep, another busy, happy day behind him. Easiest to find herself catching Alexis's eye in amusement at some remark that brought a smile to grown-up lips, or at the intense pleasure Nicky took in his games and play, or, most moving to Rhianna of all, when he would spontaneously show affection to Alexis, the father who had only just come into his life but who seemed surely to have been there for ever.

Yet even when Nicky wasn't there she still felt increasingly at ease with Alexis—this new, different Alexis. Sometimes disbelief caught her, making her wonder whether this was really true—that all the hostility had stopped, all the distrust had dissolved away. Sometimes she thought she ought to think about it—think how extraordinary it was that Alexis had moved so far from where he had started with her, throwing a catalogue of crimes at her head with his vicious words.

But how could she think of that, remember that, when Alexis was smiling at her, laughing with her, relaxed and easy under the warm Aegean sun?

Being so nice to her.

But even as she succumbed to this new, different Alexis, she knew that there was one thing she must *not* succumb to.

Alexis himself.

She must, *must* remember that he was being nice to her not for her sake but for Nicky's. And for Nicky it was working. His happiness and confidence grew daily, and Rhianna rejoiced in it. Rejoiced that he so clearly adored his newfound father. Rejoiced that Alexis had so clearly taken Nicky to his heart. Rejoiced that he had accepted that she, too, loved Nicky so devotedly.

So why, *why*, was she filled with this strange, painful yearning? As if all she had were not enough?

I have so much! I have Nicky, and he has Alexis, and Alexis is a good father, who trusts me now. I have no reason, no reason at all, to feel like this.

But she could tell herself that all she liked; it did no good. The truth still stared her in the face. With every smile Alexis bestowed on her, with every laughing moment shared, with every little skip her heart gave, with every covert glance she gave to him—drinking in the way his long, bare legs braced against the hull as he tacked the dinghy, the way his long fingers curved around the stem of his wine glass, the way his polo shirt moulded to his muscled shoulders, the way the water dazzled like diamonds on his sea-wet glistening torso, the way the wind winnowed his hair as he sat at the wheel of the motor boat, guiding Nicky's steering—with every moment, every minute she spent with him she knew, with a deep, helpless sense of powerlessness, that something was happening to her that she should fight with all her being, all her strength.

But she could not.

She was as helpless now as she had been the very first night she had set eyes on Alexis Petrakis.

And there was nothing, *nothing* she could do about it.

Alexis batted the beach ball back towards where Nicky was perched on his inflatable dolphin. From the corner of his eye he could see Rhianna stretched out on a poolside lounger, sunning herself. He wanted to look at her properly, but two things prevented him.

One was the fact that his son was paddling towards the ball with fell intent and at any moment would bat it back to him. The other was that gazing at Rhianna when she was wearing a new white and gold bikini that cupped her breasts and exposed her slim, lovely body, was not a good idea right now.

Indeed, letting his gaze linger on her at any time was not a good idea. Not now that her beauty was being revealed to him again day after day, as the last shadows of her illness left her, as her injured body healed beneath the warm, restoring sun, as her body regained the beauty hidden by ill-health and exhaustion.

Every time he looked at her he wanted her more.

But he had to bide his time, exert his patience. Impose an iron self-control on his desire.

But self-control, Alexis was finding, was a very, very hard discipline.

Even though it was essential.

After all—his face tightened—it had been his complete lack of self-control the evening he'd met her that had brought him to this pass. He had seen her, wanted her, taken her— an indulgence he should never have allowed himself.

He would not do so again.

No more mistakes, he had promised. He could not afford any more.

Because the stakes he was playing for were far, far too high.

This was his last chance, and he must play it very, very carefully. Step by step, day by day, he was getting closer. Winning her over.

Getting her to trust him.

Because only when she did, only when he had finally, finally won her trust, could he achieve his goal.

Not just Rhianna back in his bed.

Something much, much more important.

The sun was hot on Rhianna's back. She ought to move into the shade, she knew, for the noonday sun even this early in the year in these Mediterranean latitudes could be punishing.

But it was so lovely just to lie here on the soft lounger, eyes closed, feeling warm and languorous, the sun on her bare skin, almost drifting off to sleep. She would move in a moment...

'You're going to burn.'

The deep voice was admonishing. She stirred slightly, realising she must indeed have drifted off. But she felt so drowsy, so somnolent, she could not wake properly.

She would wake in a moment...

A squeeze of cooling gel pooled on her back, between her shoulderblades. She made a little sound in her throat as the cold gel impacted with her heated skin.

'Hold still,' the same deep voice told her.

And then the gel was being spread across her back, smoothed across her shoulderblades, her shoulders, drawn down the length of her spine, splayed around her flanks, across the swell of her hips. Hands, strong but supple, stroked the cooling gel with long, rhythmic sweeps into every inch of her skin.

It felt—exquisite.

She made a little sound in her throat again, and for an instant so brief she thought it had not happened the smoothing hands halted. Then they continued—lighter now, but still quite, quite exquisite.

She lay there, letting him massage the gel into her skin. She ought to stop him, she knew, but she could not. Could only lie there, her body purring, as his hands moved over her back.

When he stopped, she felt bereft.

'There. I think that was in time.' There was the slightest tension in his voice. 'But no more sun now.'

She turned her head sideways to thank him, but her lips only parted soundlessly.

He was hunkered down beside the low, horizontal lounger, his bared body damp, shoulders glistening, hair slicked back from the water.

He was so close.

So close.

Her heart started to beat with a slow, heavy pulse. Warmth creamed through her, dissolving into her.

She wanted to reach out to him. Touch his mouth, trace along the bones of his cheek, his jaw.

The pulse of her heartbeat deepened, deafening her to all the rest of the world, which did not exist...did not exist...

Only her, lying here, in a pool of sun, gazing at his face, his mouth, his eyes...

And his dark, gold-flecked eyes which she could drown in...drown in...

'Alexis...'

It was a whisper. A plea.

His eyes darkened suddenly. It was his pupils dilating, she could see. She lifted her head from her arms, reaching towards him.

Her mouth aching for his.

Time had stopped—stopped completely. The world was not there. It was only him, there so close to her...so close...

And she wanted him so much...

So much...

He started to lower his head to her, lashes sweeping down over those darkening, desiring eyes.

She closed her own eyes, waiting with aching yearning for the moment when his mouth would touch hers.

But it never came.

Instead she heard him stand up, his shadow over her.

She felt cold.

As if the sun had just gone out.

'Time for lunch,' he said. His tone was abrupt. 'Here.' He dropped her filmy sarong over her. 'I'm going to shower off.'

She heard him walk away.

Slowly she sank her face back down.

Desolation filled her.

*   *   *

Alexis made it a cold shower. A very cold shower.

Christos, *but he had come so close! Within a hair's breadth.*

He should never have let himself put gel on her back.

But he hadn't been able to resist. She'd looked so tempting there, spread out beneath the sun. Nicky had been borne indoors by Karen to get changed for lunch, and he had seen that Rhianna was falling asleep in the midday sun.

And he hadn't wanted her burning...

He wanted nothing getting in the way of his purpose now.

He sluiced the chilling water over his shoulders.

Only one more day to go now. He could last that long.

He would have to.

But it was good, he realised as he turned off the shower and snaked a towel around his hips, taking another to dry his hair with. Good that it had happened—that incident by the pool. It proved to him that she was ready—very, very ready. Oh, he had no worry that he could not do what he intended with her—that night five years ago had proved that.

But having her make that soft, sensuous moan in her throat, gaze at him like that just now, mouth parted, waiting for him to kiss her, had been too close a call.

If he had lost his self-control and kissed her—

Could I have stopped?

He didn't need to answer.

By the time Rhianna joined the lunch table she was composed again.

She had forced herself to be.

She had received a message. Loud and clear. She was Nicky's mother. Nothing more.

She had to accept it.

Just as she'd had to accept that five years ago she had been a one-night stand.

It didn't matter was what happening to her now. It didn't matter that with every day that passed her emotions were getting more and more tangled. It didn't matter that when Alexis smiled at her her heart lifted.

Because there was one reason and one reason only why he was being nice to her like this.

For Nicky's sake.

He had spelt it out to her, made it clear right from the start. Even when he'd been throwing his vileness at her it had been for Nicky's sake. For Nicky's sake he had been prepared to tolerate her in his son's life though he'd thought her a drug-addict and a gold-digger. And for Nicky's sake he had been prepared to be civil to her, make his wretched rapprochement with her, even though he'd thought she had used her body to persuade him to approve the takeover of her father's company.

And even though he now accepted that he had 'misinterpreted' her behaviour that night—even though he had told her he had no more tests for her to pass—even though he was now being so extraordinarily *nice* to her—nothing else had changed.

It was all still for Nicky's sake.

And how can I complain? How can I complain that Nicky is the most important person in his father's life when he is the most important one in mine?

The only one.

The only one I care about.

But even as she thought it she knew it for a lie.

CHAPTER TWELVE

'I HOPE you will not object, but I have told Nurse Thompson and Karen to take some time off. They've been on duty continuously, and Karen is missing her boyfriend in England and Nurse Thompson tells me she would like to see something of Athens while she is here.'

Alexis set down his coffee cup and looked across at Rhianna.

She had changed into the creamy sundress that he had told her matched her hair. Its colour flattered her, as he had known it would, setting off the honeyed tan of her skin exposed by the tiny shoestring straps.

She was slightly tense, he could see.

But then, so was he.

That incident by the pool was not easily banished from his mind.

But it was essential that he put it from him—and that she do likewise.

The clock was ticking. Getting the nurse and nanny off the island meant that tomorrow evening he could make his move.

He needed Rhianna completely off her guard.

No time to mount any resistance to him.

No time to do anything but provide him with the proof he needed.

Rhianna nodded, giving an uncertain, flickering smile. Lunch had been awkward, even with Nicky present as well as Nurse Thompson and Karen. And now that Karen had whisked a protesting Nicky off for his nap, and Nurse Thompson had disappeared into her quarters, she felt yet more awkward.

She knew she mustn't. Knew that the awkwardness was entirely of her own making. Alexis was behaving with her as he had been doing for days now. There was nothing different about it.

And she must take her cue from that. Forget about that moment by the pool. Put it out of her mind. Not think about it again.

She must not ask for more—she had so much.

She must appreciate what she had. Appreciate Alexis being nice to her...

It was, after all, so much more than she had ever thought possible.

It must be enough.

Even if it wasn't.

But what was the point of crying for the moon? None.

Resolutely she answered him, trying to make her voice sound relaxed.

'Um—yes, of course. You're right—they haven't had any time off at all yet. When—when will they be going?'

'I thought tomorrow. They can go back to Athens with the helicopter—in time for Karen to get a morning flight to London and Nurse Thompson to start her sightseeing. My office is sorting tickets and hotel accommodation, respectively—which I will provide. I think they both deserve that, don't you?'

'Yes, indeed,' Rhianna replied warmly. 'They've been wonderful—both of them.' She looked across at him. 'It's very generous of you,' she said.

It was difficult to meet his eyes, but she did it all the same.

'Will you be able to cope without them?' he asked. He gave her a questioning look. 'I don't want their absence to set you back.'

She felt the colour run slightly into her cheeks.

'You know, I really don't need nursing any more. I know what pills to take, and I do my physio exercises every morn-

ing. And I feel bad at having Karen here still, too. Now that
I'm better I can take on looking after Nicky again.'

'So you want me to sack them both?' Alexis enquired, his
eyebrows rising quizzically.

'No!' Rhianna riposted. 'It's just that I don't want you
spending money you don't have to.'

Something flickered in his eyes. Then it was gone. She
wondered if she'd imagined it. Then he was speaking again.

'Well, let us see how we manage without them while they
are away,' he said temperately.

For a second that expression was in his eyes again.

Then it was gone.

The villa seemed very empty without Nurse Thompson and
Karen. Even though Maria and Stavros were still there, they
were busy with their duties as usual, and it was almost,
Rhianna thought, as if there were only she, Nicky and Alexis
on the island.

It felt strange.

It made her, she knew, even more aware than ever of
Alexis—being all on her own with him with Nicky.

Or was it just because the scene by the pool kept haunting
her, playing itself over in her mind, making her feel so aware
of him?

She wished she didn't. Wished she could just accept him
for what he was—the father of her child. A child who needed
both parents to love him, cherish him, to make his world safe
and happy.

And we're doing that, she thought. Nicky is happy—safe
and secure.

She still could not see the future, but surely now that
Alexis no longer had reason to think so ill of her they could,
in time, work something out? Surely that was possible now?

But what it could be she did not know. She and Alexis
were separated by so, so much—nationality, wealth, back-
ground.

Into her head stole a memory. The evening when she had voiced questions about Nicky's future.

We get married he had said...

It had been a test, nothing more. A last demonstration of his mistrust of her.

She knew that. He had said so himself.

But supposing it hadn't been. Supposing he really, really had meant it. That they get married...

No. Stupid. Impossible. Insane.

Marriage was more than making a home for a child.

Much more.

The scene by the pool played again.

Alexis pulling back. Walking away. Rejecting her.

She felt heat flush through her, then cold.

No. Whatever they worked out about Nicky's future, it would not include marriage.

Alexis sat out on the terrace nursing a cold beer. Inside, Rhianna was settling Nicky to sleep.

He felt his tension rise. This was it. Tonight he would get the proof he needed.

The proof he had to have.

There was a footfall behind him. He got to his feet.

She was there.

His breath caught.

Christos, *but she looked stunning—*

She was wearing another of the outfits he had had delivered for her. It was a deep jewel-like turquoise colour, a loose, long-sleeved top in a chiffon material threaded with silver, a flowing, floating scarf wound about her neck, and matching long, loose trousers. Her unfettered hair framed her delicate jawline. She wore no make-up and did not need a scrap of it, Alexis thought. Her rare natural beauty needed no adornment.

His desire was instant. Overwhelming.

But he would have to staunch it. Hold it in check.

For just a little longer.

She took her place. She seemed—tense, he registered. Was finding it difficult to meet his eyes. But then she'd been like that all day. Well, that was all to the good now. He *wanted* her aware of him. Vulnerable to him.

It was exactly the way he wanted her.

He sat down again, and right on cue Stavros arrived, bringing the champagne.

'*Kyria, kyrios*—' He flourished the tray and deposited it on the table.

Rhianna's eyes widened.

'Champagne? Why?'

'To celebrate,' returned Alexis.

'Celebrate what?'

But he did not answer. Only let a smile play briefly on his lips before turning his attention to Stavros and exchanging something with him in Greek. The man nodded and replied, then set about opening the champagne. The cork flew off over the beach with a loud pop, and then Stavros was filling up the glasses. When he had done, he said something again in Greek and took his leave.

Alexis picked up his glass.

He paused expectantly. Still feeling bemused, Rhianna lifted her glass to her lips. The cold liquid effervesced on her tongue. Her eyes met Alexis's across the table.

Their obsidian depths were flecked with gold—pure gold...

And suddenly, out of nowhere, memory speared through her.

Alexis looking at her, those magnetic night-dark eyes holding hers as she drank his champagne.

Five long years ago on the night that had changed her life for ever.

And now she was drinking his champagne again.

An ache overcame her, a low, agonising ache that made her fingers clench around the long stem of her champagne flute. Abruptly, she raised it to her lips. The pale, cold, effervescent liquid beaded in her throat as it slid down.

It should have dulled the ache. But it did not. It seemed only to make it pierce her more. Of their own volition her eyes went to the man sitting opposite her. She could not help it.

He was so devastatingly compelling. She wanted to gaze and gaze, stare and stare. The crisp sable hair, the strong nose, the carved planes of his face, and the eyes—oh, the eyes! Veiled, unreadable, obsidian flecked with gold. For one long, aching moment she let herself gaze into them.

Something flickered. Deep, deep within.

And then with another flourish Stavros was coming out again, this time bearing a tray filled with tiny bowls. *Mezes,* Rhianna recognised. Traditional Greek delicacies—olives, stuffed vine leaves, tiny deep-fried cheese pastries…

By the time he had set them all out she had recovered. And as she sipped her champagne and nibbled at the myriad of dishes she made herself talk. The kind of things they had talked about in these last days—ordinary, everyday things: Nicky, Greece, world affairs, films, music, books, food. Easy, unexceptional conversation. The kind she had got used to now with Alexis. He had always taken the lead, and she had been too bemused by the new, different Alexis he had become towards her to do anything other than follow where he led.

Yet tonight, she fancied, it was *her* taking the lead, not him. She who prompted his answers with another question, and another…

Mezes consumed, Stavros went on to serve their main course: tenderly baked lamb that melted in her mouth, washed down with rich red wine.

Somehow she got through the meal. Somehow she managed to sound normal.

And all the while the ache inside her grew and grew.

Stavros emerged one last time, placing tiny cups of iced

sorbet in front of them and setting down a tray of coffee—
the customary combination of filter for her and Greek for
Alexis. Then he set out cognac for Alexis. Rhianna declined
a liqueur, as she always did.

She had drunk both champagne and wine. They should
have numbed her, she thought. Yet they seemed only to have
made her yet more vividly aware of Alexis. She knew she
shouldn't be. Knew it was stupid, pointless, insane to let
herself react to him like this. But she could not stop.

She drank him in. The way his long, supple fingers held
his cup, lifted his glass, gestured to make a point as he spoke.
The way the strong column of his throat was framed by the
collar of his open-necked shirt. The way the planes of his
jaw, his cheekbones, seemed to incise the night. The way his
dark hair shadowed his head. The way his mouth tugged
slightly at one corner. The way his long black lashes swept
down over those deep, glinting eyes.

It was as if she were more vividly aware of him than she
had ever been.

Except for that one fatal night, so long ago...

The ache pierced at her, stabbing with pain.

She drank her coffee, dutifully taking sip after sip. Conversation ebbed, died away. She had no heart to try and start
a new topic. Across the table, she watched Alexis slowly
swirl the brandy in his glass.

Then, as if aware of her watching him, he set it down.

'Come down to the sea's edge,' he said. 'The stars are
particularly clear tonight.'

He got to his feet, crossing to turn off the light on the
terrace. Rhianna blinked, letting her eyes adjust. Slowly she
got to her feet, following him to the top of the flight of steps
that led down to the beach.

'Can you manage?' he asked.

She nodded, then murmured, 'Yes, thank you.' She walked
down the steps beside him. His sleeve brushed against hers.

The ache came again, more piercing.

At the foot of the steps she slipped off her shoes. It was easier to walk in bare feet. The sand was cool beneath her soles, and beyond the shelter of the terrace she felt the whisper of a breeze on her, but it was not cold. Even so, she redraped her scarf around her and looked upwards as she walked down to the sea at Alexis's side.

The stars were, indeed, exceptionally clear tonight. The moon had not risen yet, and the sky was a fretwork of gold and black. As they drew further from the villa the stars' brightness increased.

At the sea's edge Alexis halted. He stood, head lifted, gazing upwards.

For a moment there was silence as they both gazed at heaven's floor.

'I'm not very good with stars,' Rhianna murmured.

Alexis lifted an arm.

'The Plough,' he said, pointing to the northern sky above the villa's roof. 'The two pointer stars, showing where the North Star is. Can you see?'

'I think so,' she answered.

'And Cassiopeia—can you see the constellation shaped like the letter W?'

'I'm not sure. Who was she? She sounds Greek.'

She was making conversation. She knew she was. But she had to. She was standing here, on a night-dark beach, beneath a sky full of stars.

With Alexis.

And all she must do was talk about constellations, Greek myths, heroes and heroines. Because that was all he wanted to do. To show her the stars.

Nothing more.

The ache came again. Deeper than ever. In the very core of her being.

'The mother of Andromeda,' answered Alexis. 'The princess whom Perseus rescued from the sea monster.'

'I thought he slew the Gorgon—Medusa?'

'That too.'

'I can't see it. The W shape.'

'There.'

He moved behind her, his hands resting lightly on her shoulders for a moment as he positioned her.

Electricity ran through her. Then it was gone.

She tried to focus on where he was pointing, but the stars just seemed a confused mess. She lowered her head from staring heavenward, feeling her neck unstiffen.

Alexis was not looking at the stars.

He was looking at her.

And suddenly, out of nowhere, the electricity was back—prickling through her nerves, her flesh.

She couldn't move.

Was held like a statue, like a nymph caught by a god.

He reached out a hand to her. Curved it around the nape of her neck, beneath the fall of her hair.

Her breath stopped. Her lips parted.

He drew her to him, lowering his mouth to hers.

His kiss was slow, and soft, and she could taste the cognac on his lips.

Slowly, very slowly, she felt her body melt.

His free hand slid around her waist, drawing her closer to him.

He went on kissing her.

Over her head the stars wheeled in a slow, dizzying arc. She felt her body sway, weak and boneless. He pressed her closer to him. She clung to him, her arms going around the strong column of his body, feeling its hard, muscled strength beneath her palms.

The kiss went on and on, endless and sweet and melting. His mouth was like velvet against hers, and she felt her lips part to his.

Wonder drenched through her. Wonder and disbelief.

Alexis was kissing her. Softly, sweetly, languorously.

Moulding her body to his, taking her softness to him, holding her against the warmth of his broad chest, his narrow hips.

It seemed an eternity of time, and yet when he released her mouth, but not her body, folding her still against him, the stars had not moved at all.

She felt his fingers still cupping her nape, stroking in her hair as he gazed down at her. She gazed back, lips parted, eyes distended, weak and bemused.

'Alexis…'

She breathed his name. It was a question, a confusion, a wonder.

Softly he brushed her lips with his.

'Shh—no words, no words…'

He murmured something in Greek to her, soft and mellifluous. Her eyes were melting into his. She felt herself fall into their depths in a slow, arcing curve, and drown…drown deep within.

He kissed her again and she was lost. Giving herself to the sweetness, the wonder of it. Alexis…kissing her.

He would not let her speak, hushing her mouth with his. Not even when he had swept her up into his arms and taken her back inside, laid her down on her bed in the deep, concealing darkness of her room.

'No words,' he said, and his mouth found hers again.

It was wonder and bliss. Soft, slow sensuousness. He eased the tiny straps of her sundress, his mouth gliding over the swell of her breasts, making her lips part with the sweetness of sensation, felt the tips of her breasts bud like ripening flowers under his lips, his slow, circling tongue.

Time ceased. Ceased to exist. Nothing existed. Only the touch of his mouth on her. Only the soft, slow caresses of his lips. His gliding, stroking hands as they eased clothes from her, from him. Only the sweet drowning of her body, the honeyed, sensuous bliss as his body moved on hers.

She felt the strength of his bared shoulders, the leanness of his smooth, muscled flanks, the long, powerful sculpture of his spine, his back, spanned by her hands, caressed so wonderingly by her fingertips in the velvet darkness of the night that cradled them. She felt her body arch and move to his, her face lift to his, her mouth yearn to his. She heard him murmuring to her in soft sibilance, the words unknown but the voice a caress, a kiss. She felt his strong hands smooth her thighs, felt him moving them with his, and all the while the murmuring voice, the velvet mouth. Her arms wound around him, holding him to her. She was cleaving to him, his body to hers, her body to his, becoming one, easing together, fusing with slow, infinite sweetness, a honeyed melting into one flesh, taking him into her, into her very core, her very being.

And then, as he moved within her, she felt the sweetness ripen, swell within her, grow and intensify, distilling into something so wondrous, so miraculous, that her lips parted with a faint, high sound, her eyes closing upon themselves. Her hips were straining against his, her thighs taut against the fusion of their bodies, her hands splayed around his back as she gave herself to her body's consummation.

And to his.

She felt his body tauten, every muscle fast against her tighten and hold for one long, endless moment. And then release—release with a slow, inexorable power, filling her, completing her, so that the same blood flowed through their veins, the same heart beat in their breasts.

On and on while she clung to him, neck arched, her body still fused to his, fusing his to hers.

On and on until she felt her body slacken, and his. The fusion ebbed, and the honeyed sweetness, and she lay quiescent, spent, within the cage of his arms, blindly gazing up at him in the darkness.

Beyond everything but wonder.

She felt him shift, felt his arm reach and click on the light, then dim its glare to a soft glow.

But his eyes, as they gazed down at her, were dark, dark pinpricks.

'Proof,' he said softly. 'Absolute, incontrovertible proof. You've played right into my hands at last.'

Triumph blazed in his face.

And suddenly Rhianna knew exactly what had happened. A cold, icy hand clutched at her heart, squeezing it tight. Oh, yes, she knew exactly what had just happened.

She had just had sex with Alexis Petrakis.

And fallen right into the trap he had set for her.

The test he had set for her.

The test she had just totally, spectacularly failed.

The cold iced through her, freezing her blood, her flesh.

Her mind seemed to have parted from her body. It had cut free, and now she heard it speak to her. Each word a blow. Mortal. Lethal. Deadly.

It had been another test. All of it. Everything. Just another test. The flowers, the clothes, the smiles. All the 'niceness' to her, day after day.

Just bait, that was all. Bait to set a trap—a trap he'd sprung tonight.

A test.

The last one left to him.

She had left him, she knew, no other option.

So what else had he had to fight her with?

He had gone for her one helpless weakness.

Himself.

And she knew exactly why.

He had just said so.

He'd needed proof.

And she knew exactly what for.

The pain of it crippled her. Lacerated her like talons in her flesh.

She stared up at him.

'My God,' she breathed. 'You bastard!'

She pushed him with her hands—violently, roughly.

But he had jackknifed up, his face contorting as he pulled out from her in a short, sharp movement.

'*What?*'

She rolled sideways instantly, away from him, taking the sheet with her to cover her nakedness. Her treacherous, betraying nakedness. He tried to draw her back.

'Don't touch me!'

His face changed.

'Don't touch you? After what just happened? *Thee mou*, but I have all the proof I need. Don't try and deny it.'

Her eyes spat at him. Her throat was being garrotted.

'I don't care. You're not getting him. You're not taking him from me! You can go to your tame judge and tell him about your bloody *proof*, but I don't care. I'll fight you. I'll *fight* you—you'll never take Nicky from me. Never, never!'

She could hear the hysteria in her voice but didn't care. Didn't care about anything except Nicky—her son, her son—and this vile, hideous man who was still, *still* trying to take him from her. Still trying to test her, trap her, so that he had the *proof* he needed.

Proof she was an unfit mother—

'Are you insane?'

His words cut right across her. Stunned, disbelieving. For a moment he just stared at her, shock etched in his every feature.

'*Thee mou*, is that what this is about?'

Her face contorted.

'Don't give me that—you know it is. You planned it. I know you did. You couldn't get any other dirt to stick on me so you resorted to this!'

His eyes flashed black fire.

'To *what?* In God's name, Rhianna—'

'To *this*. Sex. *Sex!* It's all the dirt you had left to pin on me. You set this whole thing up because it's all you had left! You couldn't nail me any other way! I wasn't a drug addict,

I tore up your filthy cheque, and I shot down your attempt to get me to say I wanted to marry you. That left you with one thing and one thing only! To try and prove I was unfit to be a mother because I was a woman who'd roll into bed with any man at the drop of her knickers. You threw that at me the first time you hurled your foul accusations at me, telling me you were going to keep Nicky, and now you've gone and proved it. I fell—wham, bam—into bed with you tonight exactly the same way I did five years ago, and you're boasting to me that you've got the proof you wanted! And now…' She took a choking, shuddering breath. 'Now you'll use it to try and take Nicky from me. But I won't let you— I won't—'

He seized her shoulders. Hands like steel gripped her.

'Enough! I will not hear this. I will not even listen. But you—you will listen. Rhianna—listen. *Listen* to me. This was not a trap—a test. Yes, I wanted proof—but of something quite, quite different.'

Her face contorted.

'I *trusted* you, Alexis, I trusted you. You'd convinced me—you know that? Convinced me you really were genuinely trying to be nice. But all that niceness, all those smiles that you poured over my head like syrup these past days, you didn't mean any of it, did you? *Did you?* It was all just hogwash! Worse than hogwash. You were stringing me along, setting me up—setting me up for this! Weren't you? *Weren't you?* You had the whole thing planned, didn't you?'

She saw the truth of her accusation in his face, and she felt sick—sick to her core.

'No—it wasn't like that. Believe me, Rhianna. That's all I ask of you—believe me. You *must* believe me!' His eyes flashed. 'You have my word—it is not as you think.'

She reared back, clutching the sheet to her. Her face whitened.

'Oh, God, you have a nerve. You want me to believe you? Well that's more than you ever did me.'

Emotions were churning away inside her, a tangled, tumbled mess. But one—one was surfacing. Powerful and bitter.

'When did you ever believe *me*?' she demanded. 'Never!'

He had thrown so much at her—one vile accusation after another—and when had he ever believed her when she had denied them?

'You condemned me from the moment you knew I had borne your son—and you never believed a word of *anything* I said in my own defence. Not once. You assumed I was after your money the *whole* time, one despicable way after another. Though I told you I didn't want a penny of it. That all I wanted was Nicky. But you went right on anyway, didn't you? Testing me for greed time after time. You dangled marriage in front of me to see whether I'd snap it up like a grasping little gold-digger. You—'

'No!' He seized her hands fiercely. She tried to yank them away, but his strength was too great for her. 'You thought it was that—but it wasn't. I swear to God it wasn't! It was because—'

'And that obscene offer of twenty million pounds in exchange for Nicky—you admitted it—you admitted that you were testing me out.'

He let go her hands. Dropped them into her lap.

'That I cannot deny.' He drew breath, sharp and hollow. 'I had to find out—find out if my son had a mother who would sell him for hard cash.'

She looked at him. Her eyes were very clear when she spoke. Her words were very clear.

'You thought me a drug addict—but addicts can love their children. You thought me no better than a whore—but whores can love their children. You thought me vindictive enough to keep your son from you—but mothers who do that can love their children. My God, murderers can love their children!' Her voice rose. 'But what cause had you to think

I was lower than any, *any* of those? That I would sell my child for cash? *What mother would do that?*'

For one long, endless moment there was silence.

Then, into the silence, he said, 'My mother.'

CHAPTER THIRTEEN

THE air in the room froze. She could feel it happening. It was as if something evil had entered.

Then she heard his voice again. There was no emotion in it. None.

None in his eyes. His face.

'My mother sold me. She sold me to my father when I was five years old. It was for ten million pounds. A large amount in those days. That was the price of her divorce settlement from him. Had he refused, she would have fought his attempt to get custody of me through every court in Europe. She'd have won, too. Every judge she'd have come up against would have found in her favour. You see, she was a doting mother. Absolutely devoted. I was her darling, adored baby. She lavished hugs and kisses on me. I was the apple of her eye. At least when anyone was looking. Anyone who needed to be impressed, that is.

'In front of the staff she did not need to be so devoted. Nor in front of her lovers. The trouble was it was not just those whom she needed to impress who were fooled by her devotion. I was fooled as well. So when she sold me to my father I did not understand why he would not let me see her again. He told me then that I would never see her again and I didn't. It made me hate him. So he told me what she had done. Then I hated her, instead, and loved my father. But he didn't want my love. And he never gave me his. Because the day she took his cheque for ten million pounds my mother also informed him that I wasn't his son, but the child of one of her legion of lovers. He only kept me to save his face, so that he would not be laughed at for having not just a wife who'd walked out on him but one who'd cuckolded him and sold him the resulting bastard for a fortune. He told me so on his deathbed. They were his last words to me.'

He fell silent. The air was too thick to breathe.

And yet she could see—see with crystal clarity.

See everything. Everything that she had not seen before.

Understand what she had not understood before.

That everything Alexis had done had not been to protect Nicky from her—but from his own mother.

The demon who still haunted him.

She looked at him. He had drawn away from her. Lain back down again, his eyes staring up at the ceiling. Seeing nothing. Remembering everything. Every last drop of pain.

Related with such dispassion.

A dispassion that reached inside her and crushed her heart with horror.

Her hands were pressed to her mouth. Her throat was so tight she could have snapped it like frozen wire. And her breath was hollow in her lungs.

'Oh, God,' she said. 'Oh, God.'

Then slowly, very slowly, she lowered her hands from her mouth and reached for his hand, lying inert by his side. She held it very tight, pressed between her hands.

A great wave of compassion and pity and understanding went through her. And more than that—forgiveness.

Because to understand all was to forgive all. Understanding just what demons drove him, why he had subjected her to all that he had, allowed her to wash it all away.

'I understand now.' She spoke quietly. 'I understand why you did what you did to me. I understand why you thought the worst of me, why you dared not believe me innocent of what you accused me of, why you had to go on and on trying to show me up, catch me out—test me.' She paused. 'But you don't have to test me any more, Alexis. Truly, truly you don't. I am not your mother any more than you are my father—or your own. Their cruelty, their callousness, their unspeakable selfishness is not in us. Nicky will never suffer as you suffered. You see—' Her throat caught. 'He has us to love him, keep him safe.'

She took a breath and said what she knew she must say to end, finally, this unbearable war between them.

'I want to share custody with you. Nicky is your son and mine. Now that I know what drove you to distrust me so much, so that you had to do everything you could to protect him from the woman you feared I was, I can trust you. Trust you not to try and take him from me.'

She looked down at him. Tears were pooling in her eyes.

His eyes, seeing now, were resting on her. There was an expression in them that she had never seen before, but it made the tears pool more.

'Why?' he said softly, his voice as strange as his eyes. 'Why would I want to take my son from the woman who above all else I would choose to be his mother? Yes, I was haunted by what had happened to me—and it made me fearful that you would prove the same as my mother, as cruel and heartless. But you are as different from her as night from day. Your love for Nicky shines like a star in heaven. And you have endured so much for him—at my hands. I cannot bear to think of it. Do you not know how much I regret having done what I did to you?'

His eyes searched her face.

'And this last most of all.'

The expression in his eyes changed again.

'I never, never meant to hurt you tonight as I have hurt you. I beg you to believe me. Yes, it was a test, but—No— do not flinch away from me! Please listen to me, Rhianna.'

He raised himself to his elbow, closing his other hand around hers, not letting her draw away.

'I said I wanted proof, but it was nothing to do with what you thought it was. I wanted to prove something quite, quite different. I wanted to prove that what had happened between us five years ago was still there.'

Cold pooled in her.

'You mean sex.' She jerked her hand away, reared backwards. It was as if he had just struck her. 'I don't see why. I fail to understand why you felt you had to see whether you could still have me, Alexis. It certainly wasn't much of a challenge for you the first time around! From bathroom to bed in minutes. But then, of course—' her voice was unsparing '—when you're only intending a one-night stand you don't want to hang about. The sooner you're in bed, the sooner you can get out in the morning. Just like you did five years ago!'

He was staring at her.

'A one-night stand? That is what you think I intended?'

She pressed her lips together.

'It's what I *know* you intended. I was there, remember? Even before I'd opened my mouth in the morning, to try and talk about the takeover, you were saying goodbye and thanks for all the sex. The classic exit line after a one-night stand.'

He was looking at her. Just looking at her. There was something very strange about his face.

Then he gave a harsh exhalation of breath and sat up. His bare torso glistened like gold in the soft lamplight, but she paid no attention. Something hard was lashing around her heart. Why was he taunting her like this? It seemed so cruel. Hadn't they just finally made their peace over Nicky? What was the point of rehashing the night he'd been conceived? It was the future they needed to sort out, not the past.

Then Alexis was speaking, his voice vehement.

'A one-night stand? A quick, casual fling with a convenient passing female? You've thought that all these years? Dear God, Rhianna, don't you *know* what was happening the night we met? Yes, I behaved recklessly, sweeping you off to bed like that—but I could not resist you. I had never in all my life seen a woman I wanted so much, who had such an effect on me. I did not know what it was—I only knew that I could not, could *not* resist you! And you seemed as eager, as ardent as I was—coming with me to my suite. I felt that you must feel the same as I did. And, even though I know now that your reasons for coming with me so eagerly were quite different, once I had you in my arms you gave yourself to me completely, absolutely. You cannot deny it— you cannot! That was real and true—as true for you as it was for me. And I knew, absolutely, completely, that something quite, quite amazing was happening. And it was not, *Thee mou*, a one-night stand! Not for me and not for you either!'

He took another ragged breath.

'Can you really think that was all I wanted? You say I was taking my leave of you, but all I was doing was telling you when I woke you with a kiss that I *had* to go to a meeting I could not get out of because it was important to other people. Even though to me it was the most pernicious and accursed thing in the world because it was going to keep me from you for two agonisingly long hours. After which time—' his eyes burned into hers '—I was coming back for you.' He looked at her, lips pressing together.

'I was going to ask you to come back to Greece with me. What had happened that night was so magical, so extraordinary, so *precious* that I could not bear to be parted from you! I wanted to take you away with me, make you mine. Discover what this magical, extraordinary thing was that had turned me upside down and inside out in a single night! Discover, with all the hope my heart could hold, whether the night we had shared had been as magical, extraordinary and precious to you as well.'

His eyes shuttered, that impenetrable veil she knew so well closing over them. Then they cleared, looked at her again. Pain was in them.

'And that, *that* is what I sought to prove tonight. That we had not lost what we had that night—before I drove you away with my cruel words, with my arrogant distrust, my wounded anger, thinking you had made a fool of me, thinking you were someone you *never* were, thinking that all you had given me was hatred of you for being someone I would have given everything for you not to have been. To prove that it had survived—somewhere, somehow—through all these years, while you raised my son, alone and unprotected, in the grinding poverty my unjust accusations had condemned you to. That it had survived even while I let my tormented childhood make me a brute to you.'

He took a breath, ragged and uneven.

'I was looking for a miracle. Trying to win you back to me after everything I'd done to you. I threw you away, Rhianna—but I've been trying to win you back. Day by day by day. I knew I'd made you flinch away from me, made you repulsed by my touch, and I knew how much cause I'd given you to hate me. But I truly, truly thought you had accepted that I no longer thought such ill of you—had realised how very, very wrong I had been about you. I thought I was showing you that, day after day. But what I did not dare show you was how, with every day, I wanted you more and more.'

He looked at her.

'I have made so many, many mistakes with you, Rhianna. I could not afford to make one more. Not a single one. I'd already realised I'd made a crass mistake in proposing to you like that. But I acted on impulse—overwhelming impulse— as I realised, all over again, just how incredibly beautiful you are. It was a stupid, insensitive thing to do, and it made me realise that I had to tread on eggshells with you. I couldn't risk you rejecting me, flinching away from me if I showed the slightest sign of finding you desirable. And yesterday, *Thee mou,* I did not dare kiss you because I was terrified I would not be able to stop. But knowing that you were finally responding to me gave me such hope, such determination, that I knew I had to risk all tonight. I had to take you completely, utterly by surprise—sweep you away, overwhelm you, give you no chance to resist, no chance to flinch away, no chance to feel repulsed by me. I had to storm your defences and prove, *prove* to you that what we had between us we have still. And more—so much, much more.'

His eyes held hers, lambent, flecked deep with gold.

'And I did prove it. You cannot deny it. You gave yourself to me tonight as sweetly, as beautifully, as ardently and as passionately as you did that very first night. Proof, Rhianna. Proof that what was started that night five years ago is still there. Will always be there. All our lives.'

He paused. Then softly, very softly, he spoke to her.

'It's love, Rhianna. Do you not know it? Can you not feel it? It started five years ago, on our first, miraculous night together, but I blighted its flowering. Let it grow now, bringing us together after so long, so much.'

He was reaching out to her. She should pull away. She should not let him touch her. She should not let him cup her shoulders with his strong, warm hands. She should not let him draw her to him. Should not let him fold her against her body, wrap his arms around her, rest her head against his heart.

But she did.

And she should not let the hard lashing around her heart loosen to the softest, silken thread. Nor let the tears that had pooled in pity for him now pool in an emotion quite, quite different.

But she did.

She should not let the memory of that night so long ago come to her again. Nor let the shame she had felt at her own weakness in succumbing to her irresistible desire for him turn to wonder and gratitude—the wonder and gratitude that was pouring through her now.

And more—more than wonder and gratitude. An emotion far, far more powerful, more miraculous than those poured through her, overwhelming her with its intensity. An emotion she could not any longer deny. An emotion that she could only let swell through her, fill her completely, absolutely.

She could feel his heart beating, his arms around her, holding her so close, so close. Feel the tears damp on her cheeks.

He felt them too. His hands cupped around her head and lifted it away, and he gazed down at her as the tears poured silently down her face.

'Ah, Rhianna, don't—don't cry—please, please don't cry!'

But she could not stop. The tears burned from her eyes, her throat convulsing, and she pressed her face against his shoulder as he wrapped his arms so tightly around her.

'Rhianna—'

She could not hear him. The sobs were racking through her as her hands clutched at his bare, muscled shoulders. He was holding her against him, close and warm and protectively.

He smoothed her hair, her back, and then, when after a long, long time the tears finally died away, he went on holding her, looser now, but still within the circle of his arms.

'I love you,' he said to her, his voice quiet. 'All my life. The mother of my son, the treasure of my heart.'

She kissed him. Softly and silently.

Then, softly and silently, she began to make love to the man she loved.

The gold Aegean dawn was breaking through the slats of the wooden shutters in her room. *Their* room, she thought with wonder. Always now *their* room. Wherever in the world they were. For all their lives together. Wonder filled her, and happiness, and peace and joy, and above all love. Love that wound them both together, bound them both, each to the other.

She smoothed the curve of his head, tracing the taut line of his cheek. She was cradling him against her, his head pillowed on her breasts. She felt her love for him pour through her.

So long and bitter a journey they had made.

A journey she had not even known she was on.

A line of poetry came to her out of some unknown, unremembered recess.

Surprised by joy...

She felt wonder distil through her again.

I didn't know. I didn't know that I was falling in love with him. There was too much hatred, too much anger, too much distrust, too much fear.

But it was happening all along, secretly, in my heart, and I didn't know.

But her heart had known. Known better than she had.

Beneath her fingers his dark hair was like silk. In her arms his strong, powerful body lay like a child's, asleep.

He gave me his child and now he has given himself to me. And I will keep him safe in love for ever.

He did not stir. Not after so long a night of love. A night that had washed away, for ever, all that had come between them. A night that had brought them together again for ever.

Someone was shaking her shoulder.

'Mummy! Wake up! Daddy is in the way. He's in your bed and there isn't any room for *me*.'

The piping voice was rich with indignation.

Rhianna stirred sluggishly as Alexis reached for their son.

'There's *always* room for you, Nicky.'

He made more space in the middle of the bed.

His son eyed him disapprovingly. 'You haven't got any jim-jams on.'

His father frowned. 'Jim-jams?'

'Pyjamas,' mumbled Rhianna drowsily. She fumbled under her pillow for her nightdress and sleepily pulled it on.

'What about Daddy?' Nicky persisted. 'And why is he here?'

'Why are *you* here?' countered his father. He glanced at his wristwatch and groaned at the early hour.

'Need a cuddle,' said Nicky. He clambered up into the bed and with great wriggling and squirming snuggled down between them. Alexis reached his arm across them both—his son and the woman he loved.

His son gave one more wriggle and then went still.

'Mummy, Nicky, Daddy,' he said, and went back to sleep.

Rhianna felt for Alexis's hand.

'Happy families,' she said.

He squeezed her fingers.

'Happy families,' he murmured.

Then they both went back to sleep.

To dream of each other and of their son, and the long, long years of happiness that were to come.

EPILOGUE

RHIANNA stood out on the balcony, gazing out over the lake. Overhead, a high Floridian moon sailed serenely. At her side stood Alexis. Inside their room, fast asleep, was their son, dreaming of the joys of the day…

'I wanted to take you to the South Pacific,' Alexis said ruefully. 'Or at least the Caribbean.'

His eyes flickered around the lake, where the lights from other resort hotels glowed in the night. Rhianna turned to him, a smile on her face, love-light in her eyes.

'I can't think,' she said softly, 'of a better place to spend our honeymoon than in Orlando's theme parks.'

She got a wry smile in return.

'Well, I guess that's a clear majority vote,' her new husband said wryly. 'I've never seen Nicky so ecstatic. Or so speechless.'

He wrapped his arm around her shoulders and pulled her close.

'Dear God,' he said into her hair, 'how can we be so happy?'

She felt tears prick in her eyes. They came freely all the time—tears of joy, of wonder, of gratitude.

'I love you so much,' she said. 'So much, Alexis. So much that I can't believe it—not after all we went through.'

He smoothed her hair with gentle fingers.

'But we came through,' he said. 'We came through. Nicky brought us back together.'

A cold shiver went down her spine.

'I hated that social worker for what she did, and yet it's thanks to her that we are here now.' She gave a heavy breath.

'I know with my brain that she was only doing what she had to do to protect a child she thought was in danger, but—'

He cradled her head, and gazed down into his eyes.

'No more looking back, my darling—no more looking back. The past is gone. For both of us. Only the future remains.'

For one long, endless moment he went on gazing down at her, lovingly, cherishingly. Then, softly, very softly, he lowered his mouth to hers.

'Tell me, my dear, beloved wife, do you think you are still jet-lagged?' he asked, as he lifted his mouth away.

Rhianna reached up and raised her mouth to his.

'Hardly at all,' she told him, and brushed her lips to his.

'I'm so very glad to hear that,' said Alexis, and kissed her again. 'And do you think,' he went on a moment later, winding his arms more closely around her, 'that Nicky is very, very fast asleep?'

Moonlight gleamed in her eyes.

'Oh, very fast asleep,' she assured him.

'Good,' said Alexis. 'In which case…'

He scooped her up in one supple, fluid movement. She gave half a smothered cry. Then he was sliding open the glass door to the room and taking her inside.

Outside, the Floridian moon shone on.

Inside, two people, whose journey to this point had been long and painful, found in each other's arms the bliss, the peace, that only love could bring.

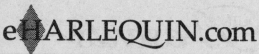

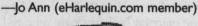

Settling a score—and winning a wife!

If you enjoyed STOLEN BY THE SHEIKH,
don't miss the second book in the fan-favorite author
Trish Morey's brand-new duet.

THE MANCINI
MARRIAGE BARGAIN
On sale in March

Paolo Mancini married Helene Grainger to save her
from a forced marriage—twelve years on he's back, to
tell her they can divorce. But Paolo is still the gorgeous
Italian Helene married. Now they are reunited, and he
has no intention of letting his wife go....

Find out how the story unfolds.

Available wherever books are sold.